PREY

BY

WENDY RATHBONE

Prey Copyright © 2018
by Wendy Rathbone and Eye Scry Publications

Cover design: Della Van Hise

A publication by:
Eye Scry Publications
http://www.eyescrypublications.com

ISBN # 978-1-942415-19-0
TITLE: Prey
Author: Wendy Rathbone

Address all inquiries to the author at:
wendy@eyescrypublications.com

Dedication

To Della Van Hise for being there for me, always.

Chapter One

The starship *Prince Fair* made the first successful raid against the Arlai.

Captain Mordecai Paronne stood stiffly on the shuttle bay deck, doing his best to hide the anger he felt at the atrocities the Arlai had inflicted on the kidnapped humans. Rage kept in check, still his fingers curled into fists. He wanted to hurt someone. Some *thing*.

Rage had never been a friend to Mordecai. In the past it had threatened to inhibit him in both his professional and personal life. He had twice been required to receive treatment for anger management. Once before graduating from Star Academy after a fight with another student, and once in a private matter involving an officer of his crew, which could have combusted into a major incident and caused him to lose his captain's stripes. Counseling, for him, seemed at best a temporary solution.

He watched as the nine kidnapped humans his crew had managed to rescue from Arla were led off the shuttle and into the bay. All were male. Most were boys that looked not yet twenty with wild, scattered lights in their eyes and mops of hair that hung down their backs. They were all naked, some severely scarred, though well-healed. But one stood taller than the rest, shining dark hair covering half his face as he walked, head down, in line with the others.

As Mordecai's eyes traveled over them, his breath caught so hard he almost choked. Not only were they scarred, but at least half the group had also been castrated. Their penises rested against hairless, atrophied sacs. That kind of violation was almost incomprehensible to him. He had to force himself not to look away as *Prince Fair's* doctor and her assistants handed out blankets.

The hangar bay lights cast an antique sheen over it all— the line of naked young men, the uniformed guards standing alert, arms crossed, alongside them—a distilled brightness catching every dust mote flicker. It was as if the ghosts of their alien captors still followed them from the rescue shuttle and into the greater star-vessel that would whisk them all home.

The first officer approached, an angular woman with distant brown eyes.

"Report, Nims?" Mordecai quipped.

"We barely got away with this lot, sir. We took a lot of fire. The shuttle navigation array is damaged."

"Casualties?" He never expected her to report about the welfare of his people first. Her love was for ships, not people, and he accepted that.

"None. We came back with only a handful of victims. But there are many, many more humans on Arla. More than original estimates, I would say."

"What makes you say this?"

"There were human slaves everywhere in the main city, sometimes whole lines of them following a single Arlai on a leash. These we rescued are from only one such train of slaves, and it took all of us to take down a single Arlai. He was that big. Our weapons slowed him, but otherwise had no effect."

There had been two other rescue missions that had failed in the past, none of them led by Mordecai. Most of the rescuers had been captured or killed, so intel on the Arlai had been sparse.

But Mordecai had seen holograms of the Arlai taken from cameras on the colonies the aliens had raided. And, he had seen them one other time, long in his past, an incident he could never forget. They were bipedal, humanoid, yes, but the majority were seven to eight feel tall with iridescent skin that appeared almost metallic, and elongated, egg-shaped heads. Their purple faces looked squashed and bloated at the same time, their small eyes barely visible amidst folds of purple flesh. Their bodies were very hard, ninety percent covered in that iridescent, thin exo-skeletal armor.

The Arlai had been kidnapping young anywhere between the ages of sixteen and twenty for decades, but not as many as Nims was describing. "How do you account for all the humans you saw?"

"Obviously they have breeding grounds for them," she said, frowning. "But not for these men. They were being publicly led on chains in the streets, seemingly sold and used only for pleasure."

He swallowed tightly. He did not want to ask outright if she had witnessed this but by her tone of voice, she had. He would read it in her report.

She continued. "It's worse than we could have imagined. I don't know what, if anything, can be done to help these victims. Some could have been born on Arla. Others more recently kidnapped. We won't know until they are debriefed. They are all so young." A rare tinge of compassion wavered in her voice.

"And the older one?" Mordecai asked.

The one he indicated stood less stooped than the rest, head not quite as bent. He was quite probably the loveliest man Mordecai had ever seen. A demeanor of grace seemed to surround him. "That tall one? He only looks to be in his mid-twenties at least. Does he show any sign of recognition, of gratitude?"

Nims shrugged. "I don't know. The rumors were correct, sir. Their vocal chords have been cut. None of them speak. Luckily, our medical facilities can reverse that damage." She took a deep breath. "And that's not all those butchers carved." Her face reddened as her lips turned down in a scowl of pure disgust.

"I see that. Have them taken to the med labs. See if their vocal chords can be repaired. And," he swallowed tightly, "the rest of the damage, if possible. When the older one's injuries are seen to, give him clothes and have him brought to my office."

He could not take his eyes off that one.

Nims nodded, arms stiff her sides as she turned. "Yes, sir."

*

Mordecai headed straight for the gym where he spent nearly an hour punching a seventy pound bag.

After a short shower and a spa-shake for nerves, he paced his small office, impatience and anger warring with morbid curiosity and a not so small twinge of fascination. The work-out and shake had taken some of his rage, but not all. Never all.

He liked things smooth, balanced, orderly. He demanded it. But the universe did not run that way. When times got tough, he had little tricks he used to convince his mind that control remained his. He meditated. He took herbs for anxiety. He focused narrowly, his ship becoming his whole world. He ran it with a stream-lined, driven protocol, his officers hand-picked, his efficiency ratings winning fleet accolades and medals for himself and his crew again and again. Despite his issues with rage and an obsessive need to control everything, his efficiency was what kept him his job. In fact, it made him the best at what he did.

But now, his blood still boiled. He ran his hands through his short, brown hair. Took sips of water every few minutes, letting the liquid soothe his tight, dry throat. He liked the taste of ship water, slightly metallic with a hint of spring wind that reminded him of greenness, of Earth. He hadn't been to his origin home in years.

The deck of his office was carpeted with stain-resistant white foam, soft on the feet. He would have preferred a hard flooring so he could stomp a bit as he paced. He wanted to hear his frustration escape in some kind of smacking sound. In short, he still wanted to hit something and revel in the echoing thwack.

That the Arlai had tortured and brainwashed these humans for their own bizarre fetishes sickened him. And yet, he was compelled to learn more. By simple duty of course, but also by a deep curiosity to look in the shadows, investigate the unknown.

It could have been me, he thought.

One of his darkest memories kept trying to surface as he paced. Since the beginning of this mission, he'd failed to succeed in pushing it back.

At age sixteen, he'd been living on the Tri-Gate Colony for four years with his father and sister, having moved there from Earth after the death of his mother when he was just eight. His father worked in the rocket yards and made good money. Mordecai and his sister Unity attended a posh private school where they were nurtured and coddled for higher education and, hopefully, greater things.

Mordecai had missed Earth more than anything after they moved. Tri-Gate was a harsh moon with a thin atmosphere and cold, hard winds. But some rare days were almost spring-like, and he and the other teens would finally get the chance to run outside for a few hours, feel the ancient, alien sun warm their skins, loving the feel of the rarer, more temperate breezes caressing them.

On one such day, when the climate warmed just enough for the children to go outside, Mordecai felt an uncontainable energy. He was a runner back then, using an indoor track to train since the age of twelve. Now he was seventeen. He felt like running forever, never to stop. He ran past all his friends, past the usually empty school-yard and into the lightly, snow-packed street. He decided he would run all the way to the rocket yards, surprise his father, and ride home with him in their flyer.

Three other boys and one girl, all in his class, decided to join him. Their parents worked in the rocket yards, too. Unity stayed behind.

Half-way to their destination, chaos erupted.

At first, Mordecai thought one of the boys had fallen and was whining about a bruised knee. His stomach dropped. They were less than a mile out. Then the screams began.

He stopped, turned and saw a silent shuttle floating overhead, triangular and winking with red lights, not like any ship he recognized where his father worked. Strange, purplish creatures, humanoid in shape, swung from great whip-like appendages hanging from the shuttle's hull. They swooped over the children and snatched them from the ground, their young, lean bodies wriggling and wailing, helpless in the long-armed grasps of the strange giants.

Mordecai's breath caught in his throat. He backed up rapidly and before he could even think, he was sprinting, slipping and sliding across a snowy field. He heard a snapping sound behind him. He made the mistake of turning to look. His heart beat hard in his throat. The alien was almost upon him, so close he could see its cold, dark eyes. For a split-second he wished for a weapon, anything to destroy the creature chasing him. He had nothing, not even a simple pocket-knife. He knew any moment he, too, would be snatched and then the real fight would begin. But then the alien's mouth turned down in a grimace, and its nostrils flared. It made a strange puffing sound and turned abruptly away, moving back toward the road. Mordecai, unable to look away, slowed. Suddenly, something tripped him up. He remembered falling. After that, only darkness.

He awakened in a hospital, body recovering from seven broken bones.

He later learned he had fallen into a natural formation, a snow-covered cave in the earth. The consensus was, after he'd been interviewed, that the alien abductors had left him behind thinking he was already dead. He'd never been able to convince them the alien had turned away, abandoning him before he fell. His four friends were never seen nor heard from again.

That was the first of the Arlai raids on Tri-Gate, but not the last. And it was not the first time young humans had been taken. Distant colonies and barren outposts, despite their defense systems, were the most vulnerable. It had been happening for years. The Arlai raided intermittently and without warning. It took more than twenty years before Earth forces had any decent rescue plan in place, and two failed missions before *Prince Fair* made the first successful rescue.

For Mordecai, everything was coming full circle. No amount of counseling and planning could prepare him fully for this moment. A line of sweat ran down his spine, an alien tendril of discomfort.

It could have been me.

He shut his eyes and focused.

The door to his office hissed open. He raised his eyelids and saw Nims. She led the oldest rescue victim into the room. She used gestures and her voice to show him where to stand. She did not touch him.

Mordecai was relieved to see the man wore a skin-suit, the usual ship's casual fashion outside of uniforms, but that didn't wipe out the earlier images of the man naked, of the beautiful skin scarred. He could not remember if this one had been castrated, too, like some of the others, and he didn't want to think about it.

"Leave us," he ordered.

Nims nodded and stepped out, the door closing behind her.

Mordecai faced the newcomer. Head down, hands clenched behind his back, the dark-haired man looked as if he were barely breathing, barely aware. His rich, brown hair was shoulder-length, but looked well-kept, not ragged, carefully cut to the shape of his face, and to enhance the delicate features of his brow, his cheekbones, his firm jaw line. The man was almost as tall as Mordecai, but much slimmer. The skin that was revealed by the suit—face, throat, hands and forearms--looked bronze in the office-light. Behind the tight skin-suit, firm muscles contracted in the arms and legs as the man moved. He was in great shape for a slave. Thin, but not emaciated.

Mordecai's eyes narrowed. Just because this man looked healthy did not mean he hadn't been through hell and back. He felt a sudden, uncontrollable surge of sympathy.

"Do you have a name?" he asked softly, abruptly realizing it was stupid to question him without a tablet. Even if the ship's medic had already structured new vocal chords for him, it would take days, maybe even a week before he could speak again.

At the sound of Mordecai's voice, the man inhaled sharply, shuddered.

"Don't be afraid," Mordecai said, stepping forward.

The man backed up suddenly, then sidled to the bulkhead, leaning heavily upon it. He brought his arms up to his chest and slid down the bulkhead, slowly sinking to his knees. His breathing quickened. The sobs were more pitiful because they were silent.

Mordecai realized then he had tried to see this man too soon. There had been enough time for treatment, but no time for even a first step at recovery. "I'm sorry." He approached the man, reaching out to place a hand on the shoulder. As he did so, he felt surprising warmth. At the touch, the man looked up for the first time, long strands of hair falling away from the smooth, wet face.

Mordecai almost jumped back in startlement, for the eyes, golden as the core of *Prince Fair's* star drive, were smiling even as the tears poured from them. As the captain watched, the man's full lips followed whatever thought had caused this reaction, and formed a matching, quite beautiful smile that lit the eyes from behind.

"I don't—" He stopped, not knowing how to finish, then caught himself stupidly smiling back, the rage inside him forgotten for the moment. "Can you write?" he finally asked. "Do you know Galactic Standard?"

With a nod, the man slowly rose. Mordecai moved toward the desk, looked back and saw the man quickly lower his gaze, look away. He held out his hand. The man recoiled as if it were a graceful dance and not true fear. The smile remained.

It was unnerving and lovely at the same time.

Frowning, Mordecai spoke. "Can you communicate to me on a tablet? Can you type your responses?" He handed him a smooth, silver board.

The bowed head nodded, his gaze coming up. The smooth, tanned face was again revealed, and eyes that fairly seemed to dance. Very unexpected.

"Come here, then."

It took Mordecai several tries before he could finally coax the strange human to his desk and into his chair. Fingers settled over the tablet's screen, slightly quivering. When Mordecai asked his name, he was surprised at how quickly the fingers moved. It seemed the Arlai hadn't taken away everything from their human victims.

On the screen, a name appeared. *Arcana.*

"Arcana? That's your name?"

The man cowered for a moment, then typed, between shudders: *Yes.*

"Was it your name before you were kidnapped?"

There was a pause. Arcana was tense, his fingers frozen over the white-lit screen. His hair hid his beautiful face again. Finally, he typed: *No.*

"Do you remember what your name was?"

Your computer system identified my DNA as Tyler Ober.

"How old were you when you were taken? What colony were you on?" Mordecai began to pace, his nervous habit. He shoved his hands into his uniform pockets. A dozen questions began to form in his thoughts. He could not hold back. "How cruel were the Arlai to you all? Did they teach you to type, or did you learn it before you were taken? Did they kill your family?" He stopped for a second, glancing at Arcana who sat very still, eyes staring straight ahead. "Are there others you know from your colony still alive on Arla?" He stopped when he saw the tears begin to line the young man's cheeks again. Arcana bowed his head, closed his eyes. His fingers lay unmoving against the tablet. When he breathed in, his nostrils widened, his lips quivered. Overcome, Mordecai was about to tell him to relax, to rest a day, but then Arcana's fingers moved. Mordecai bent to read the words as they slowly filled the screen.

I will answer all your questions. I will tell you my story. Can the tablet make a voice for me?

Mordecai reached out and adjusted a setting.

Arcana's eyes opened and his fingers moved swiftly. A soft, slightly high tenor male voice sounded throughout the room, tone artificially flat as it spoke Arcana's words.

"The Arlai are devourers."

For a moment, Mordecai did not want to hear. He wanted to shut it all out, close his eyes, see only blackness upon blackness where not even the stars could rupture his singular denial. He had been an almost-victim. He had come so close on Tri-Gate to being taken. Everything being equal, this man could have been him, their roles reversed, waiting years to be rescued, never to feel safe again.

Even having averted kidnapping, Mordecai never felt safe. Was he ready to hear this man's story?

As captain, he had no choice.

Slowly, he lowered himself to the couch by the wall. He forced himself to listen. The story was not quite what he expected.

14

"The Arlai are devourers," the synth-voice repeated. "They are all. They are the soul, somber, surreal, bringers of pain, bringers of rapture. They do not kill; their love is pure but different, not human."

He frowned at the statements. Maybe Arcana had gone insane. Under the circumstances, that would be understandable. He wanted to pepper questions at him again, but refrained and let him continue.

As if reading his mind—or perhaps Arcana had seen his frown out the corner of his eye—the tone seemed to change as the fingers typed slower and the story digressed.

"Honorable Captain of the Stars, if I am to answer your curiosity, I should write to you all I remember from the beginning of my remembrances. If this is your command, shall I begin now? Will you be able to hear me? Will you be offended at the nakedness of my truth? I do not believe I can censor my own life, but I also would not presume to compromise you or offer you any discomfort. I sense unease and would never wish to disrupt your command."

Mordecai opened his mouth to respond but the computer voice continued without pause.

"Please excuse my awkwardness; the language is old for me, from another life. I await your demands."

Arcana took his hands from the board's surface. They lay clenched in his lap now. His head lowered again. It seemed he was nearly cringing.

"I asked you questions that need answers. But I do not demand what you cannot give," Mordecai began. He found he was choosing his words carefully. He did not want to force Arcana to cringe further into himself. That would be horrible. And yet it seemed Arcana was worried about Mordecai's own discomfort at listening to the story. *I sense unease*, he had said. Mordecai wanted to deny it, but kept silent about that statement.

"If it's too early for you, I will understand," Mordecai heard himself saying, making it Arcana's problem and final decision. And yet he wanted this man's words, felt some part of himself craving them. He did not like that this felt personal to him, yet he could not help it.

Arcana's gaze met his, searching, then he typed. "Perhaps more privacy in this matter is required. I sense your discomfort. And I would be more comfortable writing my story down and having you listen to it or read it outside of my hearing."

He could not tell if Arcana backed off for his own sake or Mordecai's. Either way, a strange sensation accompanied the man's request, a new sort of burn in his veins, more than just being deferred to but something warmer, strangely friendly. As if Arcana were protecting him.

The feeling left him confused, yet hopelessly intrigued.

"Of course, that can be arranged," Mordecai said. "I'll see you're given quarters equipped with everything you need. You can send me what you have accomplished every night until you are finished."

He stood and switched on the com line, calling Nims to his office and turning back to Arcana. The man was wiping at his face with the edge of his hand. Even that gesture was done with the utmost grace.

The captain frowned, his body surging in empathy, but it went unseen as Arcana refused to look up. "Also, my name is Captain Mordecai Paronne, not—" he gestured to the air remembering the words: *honorable captain of the stars*, "—whatever that was you typed. And Arcana—" He stopped, hoping the man would look up now. Those eyes. They were so reflective of something within Mordecai himself, something hollow or hungry or despairing, and he wanted to see them again. But the man did not raise his head.

Sighing, he finished his statement in a professional, no-nonsense tone. "I also don't require you to censor anything on my account."

Nims came in then.

Arcana set the tablet on the desk, and she led him, in silence, from the room.

Mordecai took the chair Arcana had just vacated. For a long time, he stared at his tablet screen where Arcana's first words still glowed. A jolting mix of compassion, impatience, fury and wonder filled him.

Chapter Two

The sickbay's light soothed the eyes and the brain. Designed for maximum healing and comfort, it sported a soft glow to the bulkheads, and a gentling background tone of desert wind. Theta waves filled the atmosphere. The beds were pillowed and cushioned, all little square seas of soft blue and purple blankets. It was a safe space for the injured, the troubled, and the weary. Amidst all that, Mordecai still felt awkward every time he entered that domain.

The few times he'd needed the sickbay for healing, he only ever longed to leave and close himself off in his own quarters to recover alone. He had first thought it was simply his personality that made him behave this way. But *Prince Fair's* medic, Doctor Teason, told him some people were wired differently. There were those who responded with higher energy to the ionic fields of storms, and those who became more lethargic. Mordecai learned he was a more negatively charged person. He liked darkness, solitary journeys, rain, and challenge. This made him suited as captain of a starship. But it also made him different from the rest of his crew who loved light, sunshine and laughter. Mordecai liked laughter as well, but his tastes ran to the darker humors, and thus to deeper thoughts.

Now he moved forward into what he thought of as the healing womb of the ship and met Teason in her office.

She glanced up from her computer, black corkscrew curls hanging in her eyes. "I sent you my report, Captain."

"Yes, but I wanted to discuss this matter with you in person."

"Of course. My time is yours." She sat back in her chair, folding her hands across her stomach.

The room smelled slightly of mint, and something like fresh sunlight, but Mordecai's skin tingled slightly, a nervous reaction to the theta waves.

"I want your thoughts on these rescued men. Off the record. Truthfully. Can they be rehabilitated?"

"It won't be easy but I don't see why not," she answered. "Have you spoken with Arcana?"

"Only briefly. He agreed to write a report."

"His speech will come back to him and then you can maybe get more candid answers from him."

Mordecai felt a slight heat in his face as he asked, "Was he one of the ones castrated?"

"They all were, but some only with vasectomies, which we have already reversed in the ones who agreed to it. The others are being fitted for prosthetics and they won't notice a difference after awhile."

Prosthetic testicles. He shivered at the thought.

The doctor seemed to read his mind. "Arcana had had a vasectomy. He did not give me permission to reverse it and did not give a reason. His physical health is fine."

"But mentally—"

"The younger ones should be the first to bounce back to a routine life. The ones who weren't held as long should be the first to acclimate to their old lives. The older ones, like Arcana, might take longer. He was seventeen when he was taken. He is twenty-five. The problem is that the issue at hand is not black and white. Some of the boys, younger and older, uh, well, asked to be returned to Arla."

"Returned? That wasn't in the report."

"A psychology study is on-going and will take longer. It is not unusual for some victims of kidnapping to form attachments to their captors, even loyalty. "

"But the abuse—"

She leaned forward, interrupting him. "Have you ever read up on the subject? Many differing outcomes result from a lifetime of abuse, or even temporary abuse, be it simple neglect or outright torture."

Mordecai shook his head. The subject was uncomfortable for him. He'd had three lovers in his past, two of whom called him a control freak and one of whom called him abusive and broke up with him because of it. His more recent lover had been on the ship, and had left in a tumult of drama. They had come to blows, equal violence on both sides. Mordecai had been enraged for weeks. Impatient Isault had wanted more than Mordecai was willing to give, the relationship doomed from the start. He'd brushed it off as two alphas fighting for domination, but really it left him feeling somehow broken inside, undeserving of a normal relationship, of love.

He knew he was difficult to be around sometimes, too obsessive-compulsive, too into neatness, routine and achieving perfection. It was a trait he had grown to hate in himself. But abusive? He did not think he was. To him, abuse was subjugation, intimidation. He'd never behaved that way. His problem was never feeling safe after that ordeal at seventeen, and never being able to truly open to anyone.

Mordecai moved forward into the office and sat in the plush, purple chair to the left of Teason's desk. He crossed his long legs, and took a deep breath. "What are your recommendations when someone wants to return to the very horror they need rescuing from?"

"Children are not equipped to make adult decisions. Many of these young men have an arrested development and are child-like. They all may have been sexualized beyond their maturity levels and through force. That can never be erased. But they need to be educated. When they pass our health tests, they can make their own decisions. Some will make breakthroughs when they meet their long-lost families again. Others will not."

"You almost make it sound as if rescuing these people is a disservice at this point."

"No. I don't mean to imply that."

"But if we hold them against their wills—the ones who want to return, I mean—are we not as bad as their captors?"

She sighed, looking aside for a moment. The wind-sounds filled the room, giving the feeling they had been transported from space to a new world of hushed and melodic tones. "We are treating them gently. They are well taken care of. Problems will arise, of course. That is life."

"And Arcana?"

"He seems willing to be open, to give you his detailed report, yes?"

"Yes."

"Listen to him. And don't just read the report and put it aside. Look at it deeply, read what is between the lines. Look at him. Try to understand. Do not judge. That is all anyone could ask. When you have done that, you will be satisfied with this mission and all you have done for these boys."

Mordecai realized she was giving him a pep talk, not an actual report. She was good at reading him. That was what he had come here for without consciously knowing it.

He took a deep breath. This was a difficult subject. An uncomfortable subject. It involved topics of enslavement, torture, rape, sexual incarceration. He was no prude, but he was not an expert in dealing with anything like that. Yet he was the captain. He needed to know everything so he could make informed decisions. He needed to let Arcana tell him what life on Arla was like.

In the pit of his stomach a tension began, like a hard knot. He needed another round at the gym.

*

Nims entered Mordecai's private quarters without knocking. He'd been expecting her. He had just finished his dinner alone in his quarters and was relaxing. He had not yet cleaned away his empty cups and plates.

"From the refugee, sir." Nims held out a small, gold square.

"Arcana?"

Nims nodded.

"He was supposed to wave me the report."

"He did not want to send it through normal channels, seemed untrusting of them and wanted it off-line, placed directly into your hands. I guess he trusts me."

"I see." Mordecai sat forward and took the disk from his first officer's hand.

"Arcana said this is only the first part."

The tiny square felt cool in the palm of his hand, with a center of heat as if it had just come from a computer that moment.

"Sir, I feel I must inform you that when I went to retrieve this report for you, the man, well, he didn't seem—" She let her voice trail, swallowing hard.

"What? Tell me. Was he okay?"

"Sir, he was, I thought, sleeping. But when I passed by the door to the bedroom it was open and, well, I heard—" She stopped, let out a huge breath. "It sounded like he was crying, sir."

"You heard him? Has he gotten his voice back?"

"No. It was more like muffled breaths, like wheezing."

"Did you ask if he was all right?"

"Yes."

"What did he say?"

Nims shifted her feet, looked away, her usual hard demeanor actually softening. "He smiled at me, sir, and then typed on his tablet that he often cries himself to sleep, that it feels good to him, and I should not be alarmed. He said it was his way, sir." Nims blinked hard. "Sir, what those Arlai did to them--" She grimaced.

A small spot of heat fluttered in Mordecai's stomach. Panic? Or worse. He was far more curious than he thought he ought to be, but then he often over-thought everything he did or worried about.

Mordecai held the gold chip up and let the light catch it until it flashed. He sighed. "Well, Nims, I think I'm about to find out."

Chapter Three

Mordecai placed the chip in the slot of his tablet and took it with him to his bed. He lay back on several pillows and began to scroll through the first part of Arcana's report. He chose to mute the report, and not hear that android voice intone such intimate horrors. Instead, he prepared to read it at his own pace. Silent.

The very first line surprised him. This was not a formal debriefing. Arcana had chosen to address him in the form of a letter. Personal. Private.

His heart slipped a beat. He took a deep breath and began to read.

Dear Captain Mordecai (I hope I may use your first name because I like it much more than Paronne):

I am remembering some things, but not others as I write this. Please bear with me as I ramble. My memory is clear, but the order of things in my mind is not always linear. I have been with the Arlai for a long time. Things that seem abnormal to you are normal to me, and so I must remind myself to write as much detail as I can.

As I write, my old language gets better. My younger memories emerge, and some are harder than I thought they would be to examine.

For now I can only tell you my life as I think about it. You will accept my apology for not being the kind of witness you might like me to be.

The colony where I lived was called Skyover. I was seventeen. I had an older brother who called me Asshole, but that was not my name. Then, I was Tyler Ober, and I do remember that now, but that is not who I am.

I am Arcana.

The Arlai, Great Devourers of Beauty and Pain, came one day when the harvest was rich and we people were feeling full of soul.

The day they took me, they took five more boys and a girl. The girl was taken somewhere away from us soon after our arrival on Arla.

I was very scared but I tried not to show my fear. I was very angry, and planned to fight, but my survival instinct froze me. I was small for my age--even at seventeen I had not reached my full growth levels yet—and I knew I would lose and die. Still, I vowed to try.

The seven of us were put into a cage with one Arlai.

This Arlai was a male who stood very nearly twice as tall as we. He was naked, with an iridescent glow about his skin which looked hard, almost metallic. Nudity is their normal attire, but they also can wear slacks and shirts. When walking outdoors in colder hours, most Arlai wear cloaks or robes as well.

Four of the others beat and grabbed and clawed at the Arlai in the cage with us until his hard skin cracked in places and he bled blue. I was not one of the four, but I kept meaning to get up, to fight. Instead, I sat hunched against a bulkhead, frozen, watching in pure horror.

Arlai, I should tell you, are humanoid in appearance but there are differences, like the blood and the hard skin I mentioned. They also have a kind of iridescent webbing between their arms and sides that unfolds when they raise their arms over their heads. It is almost like wings.

The others tore that webbing on this Arlai, pinched him and punched him. He had long hair they pulled and large genitals, mostly pulled up into an abdominal pouch, which they kicked. We were confused that he never made a noise. His face never changed. All he did was keep trying to get up and approach us, hands out, as if merely annoyed and not feeling pain, not bleeding blue all over the hard, cage floor. He did not even seem scared. None of us could understand what he was doing. He kept getting up, coming at us, as if it were all a test.

Noley, a boy one year older than I and my friend at that time, got too close to his hand and the Arlai grabbed him hard on the arm. We all heard a cracking sound and Noley screamed a scream that went right through my body like a knife. All of us got scared then, and the four backed off. Suddenly, fighting was something that, instead of seeming like a good idea, had only brought us more agony. Noley's arm was still in the Arlai's grasp as he stood, blue liquid running down his body. The more Noley screamed, the harder the Arlai held on. Noley's arm darkened as if the blood was running into it. Finally, the Arlai let go and Noley fell back, sitting abruptly. He was crying, holding his broken arm. Then the Arlai reached down and touched his tears with his big hand. Noley flinched and the Arlai said, smiling, using Galactic Standard, "Good boy." Then he turned and left the cage and we did not eat for a long time afterward because no one came to bring us food.

Finally, another Arlai did come and take Noley away. When Noley came back, his arm was fixed. Noley did not want to talk to us about it. He brooded in a corner and rarely moved for the rest of the voyage.

It seemed like several days passed before we got to Arla.

When the ship landed, we were told by the Arlai who broke Noley's arm that we were not to speak. But we were unable to obey. We didn't know the punishment for speaking would be as bad as it was. That is the Arlai way. They tell you to do something and you do it. If you do not, the punishment can be anything, usually what you do not expect.

When we disembarked, the new planet seemed hot to us, the skies reddish, the city beyond the landing field tall, glimmering, cold. Distant silver and white buildings looked like huge, hooded beings frozen on a flat plain. That was the human farm.

They took us there. It was a big structure, not a house but more like a school, a big square building with many dormitories. We each had a bed that was fairly comfortable, toiletries, and a few toys that looked like games but we didn't understand them. As soon as we arrived, they took our clothes. They did not allow them, which was embarrassing at first, but we soon grew used to it.

The girl that was with us was taken away. Only boys were housed in the dormitory I lived in.

The first night we were still in shock, some of us crying. Other teenagers who were there, maybe a dozen, and most likely victims of other recent raids, did not speak to us at all. We could get no information from them as to what was expected of us, what might happen.

I found it strange that they would not talk. I soon learned why.

When I was caught whispering to Noley that first night, they took me away and strapped me to a table. I was crying very hard, still struggling. Then an Arlai touched me on the head and I went to sleep.

When I woke up, I couldn't speak and my throat hurt for two days.

I was kept in bed for a day with an Arlai guardian. He told me, "Your vocal chords have been cut. Do not try to speak anymore. It will only hurt you and it is a waste of effort anyway, as your voice is gone."

I remember a darkness coming in around me when he said that, the shock like a death. I tried to be a man and not to cry, but it hurt me much more than physically. I would never talk again. I could barely comprehend it.

Disobeying the Arlai nurse, I tried to scream but couldn't.

Two more Arlai came over to my bedside, nodding and smiling at my horror. It was so terrible I flung myself against my bonds and cried and it was more horrible because I couldn't make a sound. I began to choke on my crying.

They smiled more at me the way the Arlai had smiled at Noley when he broke his arm, and they told me over and over, "Good boy. Good boy."

I choked harder and I thought my agony would actually stop my heart.

Then, one of the two who called me good boy stroked my hair, unbound me and held me on his big lap, rocking me as my mother once did when I was a little boy.

I was terrified. Too scared to move, feel, even blink.

I do remember that moment in detail now, a moment I had forgotten deliberately. The feeling I had was that there was nothing left for me to do but die. I think I passed out in his arms.

The human farm outside the dormitories was like a lot of farms on Skyover. The planet of Arla has everything my old colony did: rocks, trees, weather, fruit. In the beginning we were used as slave labor for harvesting. We planted. We weeded. We did general chores and cleaning. But we didn't work all that hard. After the first week of settling in, most of the time was spent in the punishment rooms where the Arlai slowly began to teach us how to behave.

In the beginning, they spoke to us in rough, heavily accented Galactic Standard. But they demanded we learn their language not so we could speak it for by then we'd all lost our voices, but so we could understand them, and they began to speak it all the time in front of us. We learned fast. We had no choice in the punishment room.

My first lesson in the punishment room, other than learning their language phrases, confused me so much I withdrew from my surroundings and greatly displeased my instructors.

I will explain.

But first you must understand the punishment room. How it looks. How it works.

I know you want to know.

But I am tired. And it is a long time ago that I am trying to remember. If I first sleep, I will remember it better. If this is not all right with you, please come immediately to my room and wake me and I will do my best to continue my story as you order me to.

The words stopped. Mordecai felt as if he'd been holding his breath for the entire story. Now he filled his lungs. How close he had come to being one of these captives!

Finally, when he could speak, the words came out in a long sigh. "Oh gods."

Chapter Four

Early the next morning, Nims delivered another golden disk to Mordecai.

He had not been expecting one so quickly. He made sure his duties on the bridge were covered, and stayed in his office to read the next part of Arcana's report.

Dear Captain Mordecai:

I commend you for the cushioning warmth of the beds on your ship, and for the delicious meals. I woke early to fresh eggs and bacon. I have not had this sort of meal since Skyover. Thank you.

Wide awake before ship's dawn, I feel strong enough to continue this report.

I will be describing things as I remember them. I hope my accounts will be detailed enough for you. I plan to title each section I write according to the subject matter I address.

For this part of my report now, this next section will be:

The Punishment Room

The shape of this room was an 'L'. The study section was in the small line of the 'L'. This was where we sat inside big learning machines that helped to teach us, among other things, the Arlai language so we could understand when they spoke, though we would never speak that language, or any ever again. The machines taught us how to hear, read and write the language.

The machines were like giant computers you could enter. Within that computer, my mind controlled the pace I learned. It did not matter that I could no longer speak. The mental and visual and audio communion was all that was necessary. Sometimes I would also control information with my hands. I had learned to type, as I am doing now, when I was very young.

I actually liked these machines. At first I felt safe inside them. Away from the strange and terrifying Arlai. Away from my homesickness. But not for long.

The machines did not give us all the information we might ask for. Certain facts that might show Arlai weaknesses were, of course, hidden from us. But the machines could also be as cruel as the Arlai at times. If I refused to pay attention, it might hurt me through an electric shock. It did not always do so, though, so my expectations of punishment were rarely met. There was no pattern. This made me very on edge and paranoid. It was designed that way. It forced me to want to learn quickly, and I found I was very capable of that. And I still preferred machine punishment to hands-on Arlai punishments.

This is what the study section taught me about the Arlai. They are a near-immortal race who do not feel pain. They heal quickly from wounds they do not feel, and they are never sick. The Arlai themselves do not know how long they have been in existence, or even what their deepest roots are, but though they do not feel pain, they do now hunger for it and other emotions. They search the universe for their prey, as is their nature. All prey to the Arlai meet these three conditions:

Prey is mortal. There are no exceptions.
Prey is always mired in fear and self-doubt no matter how great their desire to love and succeed.
Prey is self-destructive.

Humans fit all three conditions and when the Arlai discovered our existence in the galaxy, they began their raids.

I also learned that, though they do not breed, the Arlai have four genders. They cannot be described in strictly male or female terms (though I always referred to my Arlai as "he" because of his genitalia), so I will simply state their attributes which include the physical, but are not limited to that.

The Loi are the majority. They are usually the tallest of the Arlai and have penises like human males, and very strong urges toward physical, sexual pleasure with other Loi and with slaves.

Most Arlai are Loi. They have the highest sexual drives, and they dominate their culture. They are the raiders. They are the slavers.

The K'Loi are physically like the Loi but do not have much sexual drive, and often don't even like physical touch. They are rare and stay to themselves. They can be very formidable, and tend toward physical strength. But they are more intellectual. Most seek to fulfill their emotional hunger through voyeurism. They record their species history. They are the watchers. I never met one that I knew of while living on Arlai.

The Shri are multi-sexed. They have both internal and external sexual organs, but are smaller than the Loi. They have high sex drives like the Loi, and it is said they exist in a state of bliss caused by their own unique hormones. They have little to do with the slaver caste.

The O'Shri are Arlai who grow organs according to whim. This is a talent only the O'Shri have. They can be Loi, or Shri. They can also be K'Loi. At any given time, if they decide, they can command their brains to change their gender shapes. This can take days or weeks, so they plan ahead. Maybe some of the Loi I knew or met were O'Shri, but I will never know.

The three genders other than the Loi are the minority. They are rare. They are, altogether, less than ten percent of the Arlai population. Ninety percent are Loi.

There have been no new Arlai, no children, in thousands of years. The Arlai stopped being able to breed when they perfected their longevity.

I learned all this, but I still did not understand. Why did they crave human slaves? Why us? Were we taken simply to be tortured and enslaved until we died? They could take pleasure in each other. Were they that bored with each other? Were our human emotions, and an ability they did not possess to feel pain, simply new and enticing to their ancient, mad brains?

I never did quite answer that question. And I stopped asking it after a while.

Back to the punishment room. The larger section was eerie because it was not as bright as the teaching section, and because the horrible tortures that were being done to the young men like me in there were done in silence since none of us, by then, had any vocal chords still intact. The walls were very tall, and there were no windows.

A lot of my memory of the first weeks of our captivity was about the harvesting and the language learning. But after that, when the season changed, I was sent for the first time to the non-teaching section of the punishment room. I had only ever passed by it before on my way to the learning machines at the other end around the corner. Those times I passed by are a jumble because my mind refused to accept what I saw in there, and I withdrew into myself, telling myself only the bad boys got sent there. I figured I would never need the punishment room if I obeyed well and did my work. But just when I was settling to farm work, I was taken from that. I had not done poorly. I had not disobeyed. There was no reason. But I was dragged to the punishment room anyway, and darkness seemed to grab at me again, the fear too much. I wanted to die.

My first sight in the punishment room, as I was being dragged in, was of a kneeling man, young, really, not much older than I, but thicker, more muscular. I did not know him. He was being beaten with some kind of metal wand that made a buzzing sound. His mouth was formed into an 'O' of a silent scream. All up and down the room, different young men were being tortured by the Arlai. Some were being held and rocked by their giant Arlai tormentors, only to be violently thrust away and beaten and pinched, then rocked and soothed again. I did not understand such horror.

I fainted and awoke in the arms of my own past tormenter, the one who'd cut my vocal chords and called me a good boy. I hadn't seen him in weeks. He brushed my hair with his big hands and I got angry and pushed him away. He threw me to the floor and my neck jerked back. For farming, I wore a hard, metal collar with a ring at the side and a leash hooked through the ring. No one really bothered with it as long as I did my duties. Now my leash was attached to my tormenter's wrist. I choked, nearly blacked out again until I finally leaned back, relieving the pressure. When I did so, I felt a blow to my back, then on my thighs. I pulled forward again, choking myself. He hit me again and again. I couldn't scream but my throat still ached from trying. From choking. Finally, I lost consciousness. I awoke in my bed, nearly fully healed, and the next morning the lesson began again the same way all over again.

It took me a week to learn that if I leaned into the blows, the collar never pulled. I would feel the pain of the whip, but I would not choke. When I shivered and cried and faced the Arlai with those emotions, he rewarded me by coddling me. But when I'd start to feel calm in his arms, my breathing too quiet, he'd throw me down and the whip would come again.

I soon learned to allow my fear and agony full expression as soon as I saw my Arlai tormentor, while at the same time moving toward the pain as if I asked for it. He would smile, whip me a couple of times, but softer. I learned that if I clung to his legs as he did so, the whipping was less. Soon I would fake fear to get him to stop sooner, but it didn't fool him. He stopped using the whip and went to the metal band I'd seen another Arlai use on a man my first day.

All during my punishments, I would be witness to various even worse atrocities being done to others and fear them happening to me. I tried not to look, but sometimes I could not stop myself. A man across from me, who could never seem to learn, was bloody every day from fighting. One day, I watched as his Arlai castrated him right in front of me with a quick small knife. The man fell to the floor in a faint and was taken away to medical, blood smearing as he was lifted in strong, Arlai arms. That had not happened to me and I feared it more than almost anything else. Right after that happened, I think I went into shock. I kicked and pulled at my leash in abject terror, and my collar shocked me.

I began to cry and rasp, fearing my Arlai might do the same to me in that very moment. To keep him distracted, all I could think to do was turn and cling to him, pouring out my psychic terror to him.

He smiled down at me, petted me like a favored dog, but I couldn't stop crying and he wouldn't stop smiling. I realize now that I had shown him a pure fear greater than that of being beaten or shocked. He basked in that fear and couldn't resist me. I know that now, but then I still didn't understand.

He touched me on my genitals, stroking softly, his big hands covering them. This was the first time he'd touched me there other than to whip me, and I felt only panic, and though I did not like his touch, all I could think to do after weeks of pain, of learning how to make the pain less, was to wrap my arms around him, over the webbing on his sides, and cling to him, silently sobbing. The more I did that, the warmer and smooth his touch was. It was as if he was saying by that touch, so gentle, almost reverent, "You're safe with me."

I clung to him harder, my tears on his chest, and he moved me so I could feel his large genitals pressed to my back. He was hard. I had seen some sexual touches in the punishment room given to others, but nothing too overt and out in the open. I'd seen the larger, taller Arlai get erections, but that was all. Here and now, his arousal was touching me for the first time. I was mortified, and yet he ignored my tension as his hands gently spread my legs further apart. His fingers stroked me faster, but still gently.

That was when I convinced myself. This was the one who would save me. This Arlai. If only I love him, I thought, he'll love me back and all the pain will stop.

I responded and he moved his hand faster, encasing me. At the time, being young and afraid, I was ashamed. But I am not ashamed any longer. I do not even know that emotion anymore. And so, I am not shy to admit that his hand on me was quite suddenly the sweetest feeling I'd ever experienced. Every cell in me seemed poised, delicate, fresh. It was like being momentarily reborn. I felt my whole body and mind expand as if the universe itself had entered me. As I clung to him, the Arlai said to me in Galactic Standard, "Give over to me the self that you are, and you will know true freedom."

I wanted to sign yes, yes, yes. But he had no use for my words. And he knew anyway. His command was not a question. I felt the pleasure build until I thought my skin would burst. I came hard, my orgasm jerking me back, my seed spraying outward, dotting the punishment room floor. It was so clean, so clear, this purity, this pleasure. As if I had been doused with a magic dust that sent me into a white oblivion of ecstasy. I went limp in his arms, my breathing deep and quick.

34

After a moment, my Arlai stood with me in his arms and took me out of the punishment room.

He carried me down the hall. I held onto him as tightly as I could. He entered the medical room and set me down on the table. When he turned, he had a device I did not recognize in his hands.

"Spread your legs," he said.

Pure terror shot through me. I again remembered the castrated man. I began to cry. I leaned forward and clung to him, silently begging him no.

"You'll understand soon enough," he said quietly. "It won't hurt, that's why I brought you here. That's why I gave you pleasure first. You've been good, but you see, this will ensure the place of fear and pain within you will remain open and bleeding because you know only I control you now. And the drink of it is so sweet. We need it. And you will give it. And every time, I will reward you again."

I shook my head, pressing hard against him.

"I am not going to mutilate you as that other slave was. You are too beautiful, and you have been a good slave. This will be an internal castration, little one."

I looked up at his tall form, over eight feet, at his strange purple face, the small black eyes, the elongated head. He was very ugly. But he was mine and he was going to save me. I kept telling myself that over and over in my mind.

I clung to his waist as I sat awkwardly on the table. I never did lie down. He spread my legs before him, pressed the instrument to my testicles, and then said, "It is done."

I felt nothing.

But I had felt everything.

My dignity, my honor, my humanity—taken.

I rasped in silent moans. He owned me now. I was not even a man anymore. He had, in less than the blink of an eye, sterilized me.

Strangely, I could still feel echoes of the pleasure he'd given me tingling on my skin. He had not taken that away; he had only forced me to face my greatest fear. I gave that fear to him. He drank.

He drank the fear and pain his immortal kind would never experience and found it, to my wonder, sweet.

That was when I became Arcana.

*

The report ended there for the day. Mordecai waved the terminal off, got up from his chair and began to pace. The written report had made him angry. And horrifyingly, shamefully aroused.

How could that be?

A surge of guilt shot through him, wilting that brief pleasure.

He wanted to hit something, hurt someone. Anyone. The overwhelming urge coursed through him, violent, controlling, and shimmering on the edges of a new arousal.

More shame accompanied that. But the feeling would not abate.

He actually wanted to see Arcana, or Tyler as he preferred to think of him since he could not believe the man's humanity had been entirely tapped. He had so many questions. But he refused his own curiosity, demanding from himself what he had so little of. Patience. A virtue he struggled with.

He thought about tomorrow, and the next day, when he would receive more reports. They would keep coming until the story ended. He wanted to read more despite an inward cringe. Curiosity was what sent him to the stars. Though his curiosity surged for all things, it had a penchant for the unknown, what lay hidden, what wore the cloak of forbidden. But this?

He could not get the images of the Arlai from his mind. Its bruise-colored face, its egg-shaped head, its intimidating height. He'd seen holos, seen the brief cloaked beings he'd run from so long ago, and he had Tyler's description. He did not like to think of himself, a star-farer, an explorer, as xenophobic, and yet the Arlai appeared ugly to him.

Repellant. Maybe it was because he himself had had a brush with Tyler's same fate and so narrowly escaped it.

Yet the intrigue captured him. What were these aliens doing? Why did they so badly need what they needed?

Regardless of his thoughts, humans needed to defend themselves, a not small task against aliens who could not die.

Even after he went to the ship's gym and worked out for an hour, he could not stop thinking of the Punishment Room, of Arcana, of the other slave's horrible castration, and of Arcana's own sterilization, treated as if the Arlai were giving him nothing more than a simple haircut.

As he lay down in his bunk to sleep, his dreams were haunted with Arcana's story. He could find no peace for the nightmarish flames that had began to lick at the center of his being.

Chapter Five

Mordecai pressed his hands hard against his eyes, delaying the inevitable. And yet, he also couldn't wait. The new report had arrived.

He opened his bleary eyes and for a moment felt suspended in a strangely excited yet horrified state of anticipation.

Finally, he lowered his gaze and began to read.

*

I went on the auction block soon after I became Arcana. I had taken less time than most to be conditioned to fear/pleasure, pain/delight. My Arlai was pleased. But I was not so pleased to be sold from his arms, the only comfort I had known on a hot, alien world of tortures and bliss.

I stood in a line with other young men with wild eyes and vacant stares. Some had been castrated like the man I'd seen in the Punishment Room and sported still-new scars. Others had scars on their backs and legs and chests, some older, some fresh. I, too, had scars. All healed. My Arlai took good care of me.

I could not see the ones on my back, so I did not know how they looked but I was, at the moment, not in pain. The ones on my legs and front were fresher but all healed. Because I was such a good boy my Arlai used a healing wand on me as one of my rewards for my affections to him.

I tried to ignore the men around me. All of us voiceless, we could not communicate anyway. But I did notice many of them had fear-erections. This was good for them. We were trained to show our pleasure from both pain and fear, and so they would probably be the first ones who sold.

Even with pleasure, the Arlai were careful to maintain our terror. My own erection bobbed free and cheerful, as if it knew this terrible day would bring sweet ecstasy. The more terrible it might be, the more pleasurable my reward. There was nothing I could do to hide that my body knew this fact.

When my own Arlai bid for me, I was shocked. I did not know he wasn't my original owner. In fact, he was only my trainer. But I guess I had shown him such favorable results he did not wish to part with me.

Other Arlai showed shock as well. I could understand a lot of their language now, having studied for hours a day for a dozen weeks. I heard them berate him. "Prey you train," one snarling Arlai said. "Prey you buy for your own household should not be the same prey." They called what he was doing "sinsee". The closest approximation in English is incest.

I disagreed in my mind. This Arlai was no family to me. I thought of him neither as a father or brother, only "other". Only as safety. I actually had a preference for him only because I knew him. Known horror is, after all, always better than unknown horror.

Despite the insults, my Arlai bid the highest and so bought me anyway and took me to his home.

I might have written above that I associated him with safety because I knew what he expected of me and what to expect from him. But I was still very much afraid of him. I was caught under a strange spell of being captive yet safe with him. Safe with the known. I knew if he hurt me he would instantly heal me. He would not make me suffer beyond his own needs to suck my pain. When he was happy with me, he would reward me. I did not know if other Arlai operated in that fashion, and truthfully I never wanted to find out.

I should explain that because of this known factor, along with the ecstasies he granted me that were unlike anything I'd ever experienced, I had, over weeks of training, developed an internal, programmed lust for him. I wanted him with me. I wanted to be with him. As much as possible.

Of course he trained me for just such a response. He behaved as if he cared for me. I had nothing, no one, and worse, no hope. He was all. I couldn't help but fall in love. By the end of my training, just seeing him walk into a room would bring me to arousal.

This, no doubt, had been the very reason he'd bid so high for me. The combination of fear and being in love is irresistible to the

Arlai. I learned later that not all humans, no matter their conditioning, no matter how naturally submissive, were capable of it. I was a gem in the rough, a rarer type among my kind. This Arlai had made me his own. I thought it was normal. It was not.

His beautiful home nestled in among tall, yellow trees on a flowing green hill. The structure rose dark and fairytale gothic, carved from black rock. It had small windows that let in little light. Even so, I loved it.

He showed me to his bedroom and I cowered before entering, knowing here was where I would endure the most pain, but also the most pleasure. I did not want to go in. And yet I did want it more than anything. I wanted to live here and be his and not think anymore. I did not want to have hope because every time I allowed myself to open to even a sliver of that dire longing to leave, to be free, my situation crushed that. Every time I felt that crush, it destroyed me. I wanted to just live and be and feel ecstasy again and again.

Still, I hesitated. You might read this and think my soul was broken. It wasn't. It remained whole and mine. It simply adapted. It took a different shape. My reasons for surviving became all about the Arlai, but still selfish, for I was a pleasure addict by then. I would do anything to keep that.

The hesitation came from fear alone, and how I knew that fear would please my Arlai.

"Arcana, come!" he said.

I let the fear cover me in a cold dampness and the shivers that accompanied it. It was natural now, the tart smell of ozone from my own sweat, the spice of my Arlai himself. These things were associational.

I knelt, gripping his leg. He pulled me into the room.

The carpet underneath me felt soft, spongy. The large bed, covered with white spreads and black pillows, could have been a bed in any human home, but this one was longer to contain the Arlai's height, and wide enough for two Arlai, or an Arlai and more than one human. Mirrors decorated the walls, dark, antique-looking. The room had a gray air about it that both appealed and repelled.

"Arcana! Come!" He had approached the bed after I let go of his leg. I held back. He grabbed my hair and lifted me by it. I opened *my mouth in a silent scream. He'd never done that before. The pain in my scalp burned as if open fires surrounded it. He dropped me into the mattress. I bounced once. The pain immediately receded.*

I saw my own body against the white spread—long, very clean, the color of deep flame. He had shaved my body for the auction, so my skin was smooth and clear. I noted that my scars were faint, and strangely alluring to myself. I had endured such torture and I was healthy. I could still reason, think, want. I could not speak. I could not produce offspring, but those things suddenly did not matter. Why should they? I was no longer human.

"Now," my Arlai said. "You will from this time forward know me as Blaek. You will obey my every command. You are mine now. Do you understand?"

I nodded, blinking back tears. Why, if I had resigned myself to being where I wanted and needed to be, was I crying? Because he was terrifying. Because I wanted to please and, even more horrifying, I worried I would not be good enough for him.

It was then I noticed his swollen genitals. I had only felt them against me once, aroused and pressing. But all the other times he pleasured me, my pleasure was mine alone, and he drank it in through his own psychic senses, a sort of one-way telepathy I never felt in return. To accomplish this, he breathed my scent or touched my face and head. That was all.

But now-- He was aroused. I'd seen it on occasion, but never that up close and so personal.

Blaek had a beautiful body once I became accustomed to it. He stood over eight feet tall. As I wrote before, his face was strange and wrinkled and purple, his eyes small and black, but nothing I couldn't get used to. I am describing him here, Captain, so you will know what I saw then, as if it was new, beginning all over again for me. He had straight black hair cut long at the neck and feathered at his ears, which were small, slight curves against the sides of his long head. The skin of his body was metallic but not unmovable metal, still pliant but very hard, with a lavender sheen that was iridescent, refracting all the colors of the rainbow.

Like humans, he was bipedal, and seemed to be muscularly structured like us as well. He had a hard chest with raised pecks, and arms that were sinewy, hard, long. The muscles stretched underneath that skin, always hard, always gleaming. His legs were also striped with muscle, thick, corded. Unlike humans, he had webbing that stood out when he raised his arms from his waist to his underarms, and it was soft, iridescent, filmy. For a tall, big humanoid, his genitals were, of course, large, but no more so than a well-endowed male human. His penis stood out from his body, straight and long, about ten inches. Unlike his shell-like skin, this part of him looked as delicate as my own skin, as if an inner part of him that was vulnerable was suddenly exposed, quivering in an almost shy but deviant way, an expression of yearning, pride, and lust. But also, strangely, of sensitivity. Whether that sensitivity was purely physical, or something more, I would eventually find out.

I should add here that the Arlai do not mate for children. They have no need of them. They are all sterile. But they do know sexual pleasure, of course. Their sex, to work for them, must be combined with fear and pain and arousal of their partner. If affection enters that equation, it is the most exceptional of delicacies for them. I know this to be true of the gender called Loi, which comprises the majority of the four-gendered Arlai. Blaek was the only one I ever joined with, and a Loi, so I cannot comment on the others.

I began to weep as he climbed into the bed, naked, so big and looming over me as he straddled me, his erection smacking my stomach. He pushed my legs up and my tears fell faster. I knew what was coming.

He had never done anything like this before, never used his body on me, only his hands to pleasure me. Only that. He'd penetrated me only with a long finger to teach me of more pleasure/pain.

I knew this was coming. I had simply blocked it out of my mind.

Now he pushed my knees up exposing me. He rubbed himself against my body's entrance. I froze in horror as I felt the slick.

At least there was that. The hot wetness of him. The natural slipperiness, or I might have actually fainted.

As it was, I lost my own arousal.

He did not like that.

42

"Arcana," he said, his long face close to mine, his hard body cool against my thighs and arms.

It was all so alien I recoiled. His breath wafted against my face, spicy, sun-baked from a depth inside him that must have been made of infernos and demons. The hell of his immortal condition.

His hands, which were rugged but not horribly ungentle, touched my genitals.

I did not respond.

He reached over me and brought something out of an overhead cabinet. A short whip. He immediately made use of it.

The sting of it on my chest sent me reeling and for a moment all I could see was red.

In the midst of that, my eyes still closed, I felt something hot and wet on my penis. I opened my tear-blurred eyes and saw he had his mouth on me. I'd seen other Arlai do that to young men, but mine never had. Secretly, I'd wished for it.

I felt a powerful, liquid sucking sensation and I went stiff in seconds. My hips bucked up and my mind latched onto the ecstasy that began in the back of my head and in the pit of my stomach. The backs of my thighs tingled.

He lifted his head, stroking the tip of my penis with a thick, slightly forked tongue that wrapped the top. One part of the tongue-fork delved up and down the crease there, probing the hole.

I am being explicit in this report so that you will know how lost I was. I'd never felt anything like what he was doing to me. I had never had another lover before him. If I can make you feel even the slightest glimmer of how I was feeling, maybe you can understand better how I think now, what I am.

I quivered and shook, on the verge of exploding with the euphoria of the sting on my chest and the teasing of my cock.

When Blaek could feel it, soaking it with in his breath, his touch, he moved up and his organ touched me again, slick and long, then without any other warning he penetrated me fully in one quick slide.

Impaled, I could not move. It hurt terribly at first, even with his natural slick. Despite my pleasure still coursing hot in my veins, *my body remaining on the verge of orgasm, I hated him. I wept even more.*

He withdrew slowly, agonizingly. My arousal wilted at the burn.

He repeated his oral procedure on me. Bringing me again close to utter pleasure, and those supreme orgasms he could give me.

Then he slid inside me again, hard, aching.

He did this over and over, forbidding me my own orgasm, until I was gasping, using hand signals to beg him to penetrate me and then suck me again. I hated him for this. Then I loved him. Then I hated him again.

My insides burned but I craved more stimulation like never before.

When my arousal flared at his penetration that last time, he began to slide in and out of me faster and faster, sensing my pleasure, and something inside me changed from pain to pleasure as well. I bucked beneath him. He put his long, strange head against mine. I no longer saw his purple face as ugly. His dark, forked tongue came out of his mouth and licked my tears away.

This made him groan even more. "Arcana!" he yelled. He pumped into me.

He filled me up, so big, so hard. The pain had been bad and I had thought I might be bleeding, but now I no longer thought it. My body had been trained. It molded to him. It welcomed him now.

He put his hand between us and stroked me as he had done that first time in the Punishment Room, gentle. Reverent. I came hard, the spasms never-ending as he filled me with his strange, warm liquid.

He pulled away from me, but he wasn't done.

He knelt over me, his long cock still leaking, the fluid a bluish white. He brought it to my lips and rubbed it against them. Then he commanded me to take it into my mouth.

He milked that long length while instructing me to lick and suck only the tip. Then he exploded again, after only a minute, right into my mouth. It was so much it overflowed onto my lips, chin, neck. He kept coming, threw his head back and groaned.

That was when I learned how insatiable the Arlai are,
especially the Loi whose sex drive is a constant factor. They could do
this over and over if it suited them. Later, Blaek would tell me their
drives were so strong it could interfere with every other aspect of
their lives. It was why he had become a trainer, so he could be
around the human slaves all day, every day.

Later, I wondered why they didn't just take their pleasures
with each other, and hand signaled my question.

"We do," he told me. "But we grow stale and tired of each
other quickly because we cannot feed each other the emotions we
need, not like you humans do. You are the greatest treasures we have
ever discovered."

After that first time, he held me as I continued to cry,
overwhelmed by my own pleasure, and by his. And still afraid. So
afraid.

After I had a short nap, he took me with him into an alcove
bathroom where he put me under a shower and cleaned me himself.
His hands went everywhere. "How beautiful you are," he told me.
He pinched my bottom. He penetrated me with a finger. I became
aroused again.

But I noticed he was not. I shrugged at him, pointing. I felt
fear again. Fear that I would not be good enough for him. That he'd
send me away.

"We always want the intercourse," he said. "Always. But
we control our physical arousals. I will not penetrate you more than
once a day. I do not want you injured in that way. I have seen the
ones get hurt and not recover even with our technologies to help. I
have seen them die."

He put both hands on my shoulders and moved me slightly
out of the stream of water, then licked me with that strange tongue
all over. Neck, underarms, nipples, bellybutton. He licked my thighs,
toes, and between my bottom cheeks. My erection bobbed up so fierce
it stood straight against my belly. Finally, he put his mouth there
and sucked until I rode the waves of euphoria again, swooning in my
silent, panting breaths.

When he rose, he said to me, "I drink your pleasure as if it
were mine."

And yet, his cock had not budged. I knelt, wanting to touch it, suck on the tip again. Not ashamed now, I told myself. I wanted pleasure and I wanted to live so I would not be ashamed ever again.

He brought up me. His bulbous lips cracked in a smile. "Later," he said.

He showed me back to his bed, but when I started to get into it he pulled me away. "No. I sleep here." He leaned down and pulled out a mattress from underneath. He placed it at the foot of the bed on the floor. "You will sleep here."

It had a blanket and two pillows. I was comfortable enough. But I spent more of the night crying than sleeping. Too much was still happening to me. Too much to think about and assess even then, even after months of training.

I chose to put my thoughts aside. I focused on my addiction. The pleasure.

Night after night he would take me; the ritual varied only in the fact that sometimes he whipped me first, sometimes during, and sometimes only afterward. I looked forward to it. I would come twice, once in the bed, and once later in the shower. And he always came two or three times, first by penetration, and then with my mouth on him, which I grew to crave. The taste of him was sweet, like peaches with sugar.

Actually, I wanted even more. Sometimes, during the day, if I offered myself freely, he would push me away. I would cry.

He put me outside in a cage for an entire night, and we had no sex at all. I cried and cried. I got cold. I never slept. Secretly, though, I loved the punishment. The worse the better, for my reward would match.

The next morning when he came to get me from the cage he wrapped me in warm blankets and carried me to his bed. Then he licked the salt of my tears off my cheeks and laved my body all over. He was still very angry with me for trying to seduce him all the time, but even in that state, he loved my taste. After that night in the cage, we had our first morning sex. He had his three orgasms. I had my one as he took me, and then the second as he sucked me off in the bed, not the shower, and I nearly shattered in my pleasure, kicking and panting, gripping him hard with my fingernails scraping along his hard skin.

I clung to him even after he indicated he wanted to get up. I clung hard, the tears coming again. I let my fear of him leaving me take hold. I lifted my head to him. He looked down at me with his dark, small, bulging eyes.

I pushed myself up, wrapping my legs about his waist, and then kissed him on the lips.

He groaned and drank of me for a long while that way. Everything I offered.

Then he bound my hands above my head and whipped me.

How I hated him.

How I loved him.

*

After about two weeks passed, he said to me one morning, "My leave is over. I must return to work. You may do as you like during the day as long as you keep the house neat and do not destroy anything. Otherwise, I will have to keep you in the cage outside."

I nodded solemnly. Tears welled in my eyes. I did not want him to leave. I was afraid. What if he didn't come back? I knew he could not resist my tears, so I always allowed them to freely flow. Tears were my communication. Tears were his pleasure.

He licked them away, but then he smacked my bottom and said, "Tonight. You know the rules."

We had only ever had morning sex one time, and only because I'd spent that night in the cage.

So, yes, I knew the rules.

When he left the house I knew it was because of his job. I knew he was going back to the Punishment Room to train more human boys, to torture them, to sterilize them, to steal their voices.

I know it sounds horrible, but this made me jealous. When I was jealous, he could feel it.

When he came home that first day, he was immediately unhappy with my smell and my demeanor. He did not say it aloud, but I could tell. His nostrils flared at me. He turned away from me as if he scented something foul.

When I tried to make up with him, he hit me, then he put me in the cage outside and gave me no food or water.

I cried and cried. Eventually my tears brought him.

After an hour or so, he came and got me. He reached into the cage as if to beat me. I recoiled. He smiled.

"Now that you smell better," he said, "You may come out."

I walked back into the house with him, terrified that I would do something else wrong.

"You smelled bad before," he said.

I shrugged a question.

"I cannot have that from you, or I will be forced to make you live outside all the time. Maybe even sell you."

My mouth opened in shock. All this because he had to go back to his stupid job! And because I was jealous. I began to tremble.

"Ah, that is better," he said.

When I was properly scared, he would hold me. I knew this from my first week in the punishment room, but somehow in one day of him being gone I had forgotten. He had to threaten me to reactivate that program. Whipping would not have worked in that moment, but the threat of selling me, now that was effective. I was more afraid of leaving the known and going back into the unknown than of anything else. This was how I had been conditioned. Give me the whip, or the back of his hand. Pinch me. Rape me. All of it was better than the threat of being sold to someone I did not love. For I loved Blaek, and in his way, I knew he loved me back.

After his first day at work, and my punishment, he made me eat a small meal of fruits and nuts. Then he took me to his bed. He whipped me hard. Harder and longer than usual.

Then, when I was weeping and shaking, his hard cock slicked me up and he took me hard and fast from behind.

I had no time for my own pleasure, though I was aroused. I did not come before he did. When he was done, he made me make him come two more times with my mouth.

Finally, after I was aching from the abuse, he put his mouth on my straining cock and milked me and sucked me until I nearly passed out with ecstasy.

He let me rest, then said he wanted more. He loved to drink me, both psychically and physically. So he took me to the shower and bathed me, knowing that would rouse my tired, aching body yet again.

He drank me until I could give no more. Then he picked me up and dumped me onto my pallet, ignoring me for the rest of the night.

I did not cry myself to sleep that night, but instead fell asleep with my lips curved up, tight and bold, into a smile that felt hard, conniving, aberrant.

It had only been a few months since I was taken. But I forced myself to never think about home. I loved my life now because I knew how to make it work.

*

One day, after more months had passed, usually with indescribable pain and pleasure every day, Blaek came to me and said, "You have been very good, Arcana." He lay me down on the floor of the living room, an ornately decorated area with fur rugs and jeweled walls.

He touched me all over and had sex with me right then and there. It was still before dinnertime, and he had not yet whipped me.

I had grown used to routine. I got scared. This was different. Was something going to happen to me? I always worried he'd grow bored, get rid of me. He did not have interest in other Arlai, so I knew I did not have to worry about that. But had he fallen in love with another boy? He trained them every day. It was my worst fear.

I was careful not to allow any jealousy to overtake me, knowing that scent was abhorrent to him. But I still worried. As long as my worry remained in the fear-zone, I always smelled delicious to him.

On the floor, Blaek took me hard. I arched with pleasure, then recoiled, worried again. Blaek liked the mixed reactions, and fear always got him going. He laughed, then covered my mouth with his and came hard. His cock moved in me, stimulating my own orgasm when he hit just the right internal spot. The drug of coming made me soar, then go limp in his arms. I ended up trembling, shaking to my soul, crying again. The sweet release. The worry. The fear. His laughter. The disruption of routine.

I shuddered.

Blaek licked me all over, then took me into his arms, holding me in his lap like I was a child, raising his arms a little and letting his strange, iridescent webbing swell out to enfold me which he had never done before.

He did not get up. He let me sleep in his arms. We skipped dinner, and he took me to his bed. He made love to me again. Licking me. Breaking his own rule of one penetration a day. I came hard. He sucked me to completion again. And then he let me sleep with him. He enfolded me in his webs and I found myself pressed to his hard, smooth body, so shiny I almost slid to the side. But I hooked my foot between his long thighs, and pillowed my head on his shoulder. His arms held me in place.

After several such nights of tenderness and no whippings, I learned to expect several days of torment afterward. He could not allow my fear to abate.

I had my moments of softness, of security, of feeling completely safe and enamored, but I paid dearly for them. The next day he would tie me to a chain outside and leave me, or beat me with his metal prod which also sent little electric shocks into my body. He would rape me at his leisure even when I was not ready or aroused (I didn't mind), then discard me as if I were nothing to him and make me sleep again on my mattress on the floor at the foot of the bed.

In my own little bed, I would cry through the night. Soon, Blaek would come to me, kneel on the floor by my side. "You have pleased me," he would say. "You have pleased me so much, my beautiful human." Then he would pick me up, take me to his bed, lick away the salt of fear and take his pleasure with my mouth on him. He would then give me pleasure, enfold me in his beautiful "wings," and the routine would begin all over again.

Mordecai ended up reading that report twice. He made special note of the way the Arlai had experienced Arcana's jealousy scent as extremely distasteful. It reminded him of the Arlai who'd chased him through the snowy field all those years ago. How his nostrils had flared as he turned away. How the mouth had formed a grimace. Had Mordecai been saved because he'd exuded some odor that was terrible to Arlai olfactory nerves? He'd been feeling only fear. He could only wonder what it might have been about him that caused the Arlai to sniff and turn away.

When he was done reading the report for the second time, Mordecai worked out in the gym for more than an hour, trying to focus his thoughts. When he failed, he went back to his quarters and showered cold. When that didn't help, he gave in to the urge to masturbate.

Afterwards, the guilt and shame he felt for being so aroused abated. He was able to sleep, finally, but not dreamless. He dreamed of Arcana. Not Tyler. Arcana. He dreamed he was whipping him. And then Arcana was on his knees undoing his trousers.

In horror, he woke before anything happened, but found himself aroused again. He took care of the problem, but felt guilty—for he was *not* like an Arlai—about not being able to get Arcana's face out of his mind as he came.

Chapter Six

Mordecai stiffened, hesitating outside Tyler's door. The ship's corridor glistened and pulsed with the endless white light of the bulkheads. He breathed in slowly to clear his mind. There was a faint smell of lemons on the air from the cleaning crew.

He should not have been nervous about visiting Tyler. But Tyler's reports had affected him. The explicitness alone, both disturbing and arousing, was enough to embarrass anyone. And maybe even entice—

Had it been deliberate?

He could not get Tyler out of his thoughts.

Did Tyler know what he was doing by writing as he did, what he did, in such detail?

No. Tyler was a victim. It was wrong-thinking to consider otherwise, and he clamped down on his strange thoughts.

Before he could press the chime to Tyler's quarters, Nims and Dr. Teason came around a curving bulkhead, talking softly. When they saw Mordecai, Dr. Teason called out. "Captain, I was just on my way to see you."

Mordecai moved back from the door and met them. "Why didn't you chime me?"

Both officers wore their gray uniforms perfectly, no creases. They stood straight and assured, their eyes bright with awareness. These were his two favorites, despite Nims's gruffness. They did their jobs above and beyond what was asked of them. He never had to worry with these two, and would have left his ship in their hands at any moment without hesitation.

Teason replied. "It is a matter of some delicacy. I wanted to talk to you in person."

"Can it wait? I was on my way to see Tyler about his last report." Or Arcana. Which was what the man said he preferred.

"It is about reports concerning the men from Arla, sir."

"What sorts of reports? From the rescued men?"

"No. Reports *of* the men, sir. From some of the crew;"

"Of what nature?"

Nims glanced down, her cheeks reddening. Mordecai rarely saw such overt emotions from her.

Some more crewmembers passed by in the hall. Teason stepped forward and said quietly, "Maybe we should discuss this in your office where it isn't so public?"

"Of course." Mordecai led the way to the lift. Tyler could wait a few more minutes. Mordecai did not have any specific appointment with him. He had messaged him that he wanted to see him that day. That was all.

Once in his quarters, Mordecai sat behind his desk. Nims and Teason took seats facing him.

Teason said, "These reports are unofficial, sir. For reasons pertaining to the delicacy of the subject."

Mordecai frowned. "Go on."

"One report from a crewmember who came to my private office expressed concern, sir. He had witnessed some other crewmembers with a couple of the men from Arla in one of the rec rooms. Said they looked like they were getting along but then he witnessed a playful auction of sorts." She took a deep breath. "The two men from Arla played along. About five crewmembers offered to buy the men's time. The Arlai men ended up going to the quarters of the men with the highest offers. It was only men, sir. No females were involved. Which is understandable, as the rescued men have been conditioned, well, um, to want to please dominant males."

Mordecai was furious. "I do not condone this. You know this is nothing I would ever allow if I had known."

She nodded.

Nims looked almost frightened. But she said, "Sir, the men are free men, are they not?"

"Of course!"

"They went willingly."

"They are victims. They have not yet had any time to cope with what they've been through. Their vulnerability makes it easy for them to be taken advantage of. They can't even talk yet."

Nims looked cooler as she replied, "What would you do? Cage them?"

"Of course not! But I can send memos to the entire crew. This behavior is unprofessional to say the least."

"It all depends upon who started the, uh, game," the doctor put in.

"Are you suggesting these men wanted to be sold? To be used?"

She nodded. "Their minds are conditioned to be highly sexualized. They would know that they have that as a commodity to give them survival, comfort, even luxury. It is a complex issue of mental health and consent."

"Yes. It surely is," Mordecai sighed. "I must speak with Tyler. How is his voice doing?"

"Still in progress. He came in this morning with the others and all of their vocal chords are almost fully re-grown. When I asked Tyler to speak he did not. Or would not. Nor did the others. Speech therapy will be given to all of them, of course."

"And what is the other report? You said there was more than one unofficial report you had heard." He hated stating it in this way. It was like listening to gossip, which he had no patience for. He liked his ship run cleanly, by the book. He liked accusations armed with evidence, not hearsay.

"Someone said they saw sex acts being performed on the lower decks in the break rooms that are rarely used. Three slaves from Arla were there, along with five more male crew. The crewmember who made the report left because he did not want to join in, but he said there was eagerness from all involved, and that word had gotten around that if you wanted a good time, you could go there at night and meet the slaves."

"Unacceptable." Mordecai stood abruptly. "I will be putting a stop to all of this!"

"Sir," Nims put in. "You have never expected your crew to be celibate."

"Nor do I now, but this is not a brothel ship. And I won't allow this."

"And if it were happening in more private areas?" Nims asked.

"It may already be. There should be some statement that the slaves are hands-off until they have at least had time to acclimate to their new surroundings, and to their lives as free men."

"Agreed, but running a tight ship and controlling others' freedom is a fine line," she said gravely.

Mordecai looked at Teason. "Would it be asking too much if the ship's medic made a report that these men are to be untouched, for medical reasons, for a time period of at least two or three weeks? I don't think that's unreasonable."

She nodded. "It would follow a standard protocol such as is seen in debriefings, or incidents of unknown contaminations."

"Yes, yes, it should be that kind of memo. And I will add my own words to it. For the good of the ship and the honor of the slaves and our own crew, it seems at the very least a reasonable demand."

"I will get to it right away." Teason stood. Nims followed.

"Is that all?" Mordecai asked.

"That is everything, sir."

He nodded. "Good."

After they left, he let out a long, frustrated sigh. He should have seen this coming. He should have known, after reading Tyler's words, this situation was anything but routine.

These men had been brutally raped, beaten, brain-washed. Yet he was dealing with consenting adults. It was not his business what they desired behind closed doors. Technically, to protect them, he was interfering in private life matters. But making it a medical matter helped somewhat. Still, he was worried.

*

Mordecai returned to Tyler's door. His talk with the doctor and Nims had only agitated him further. But he schooled his posture and demanded from himself all-out professionalism.

He pressed the chime, then curled his fingers into a loose fist.

Tyler stood directly in the archway as the door slid open. His dark hair hung partially over one eye. His face, the skin smooth and tanned, held very little expression. The eyes, though, were clear and gentle, and the lightest brown Mordecai had ever seen, like sweet honey.

Tyler wore a dark blue skin suit that clung to him, accenting the firmness of his body. Mordecai wondered if he should have ordered looser attire for all the slaves. He had not thought about it until now.

But Tyler's innate beauty glowed. Not even loose clothing would hide it.

He put the thought from his mind and asked, "Tyler, how are you?"

Tyler did not answer.

"The doctor has informed me your vocal chords have almost fully grown back. Can you not yet speak?"

The young man swallowed and shook his head.

"Ah, not yet." He tried to give him a reassuring smile. "May we converse with a pad then?"

Tyler gave a slight nod and moved back into his room, indicating Mordecai should follow him.

Mordecai entered, quickly glancing about and noting that the bed in the shadowed alcove was unmade, and that the eating table was littered with empty cups, a plate with the sandwich half-eaten, and two pads.

Mordecai went to the table and pulled back a seat. "Shall we sit?"

Tyler nodded and took a seat across from him.

"How are you doing?"

Tyler picked up a pad and rapidly began to compose. He handed it to Mordecai.

Please call me Arcana. I am well.

"Why not Tyler? It is the name your family gave you."

I do not know that boy. He is gone.

Mordecai looked up from the pad. "I'm sorry to hear that. Does this mean you would not want to see your family?"

No. I do not.

Mordecai watched Arcana's face as he handed him back the pad. "Your reports are very detailed—" he began.

Fingers flew across the pad's screen. *Yes. It has been a long time, but I do remember my father saying, when I was young, the devil is in the details. I have learned to be open and honest even more from the Arlai than ever from humans. Once I might have had shame. No longer.*

"I didn't mean you should feel ashamed."

Arcana grabbed the pad. *All right. But you do feel it. I could smell it on you. See it in the shadows of your eyes. You feel shame for what happened to us. But you are not at fault. So, why? You came for us. For you, this is a rescue mission. There is no shame in that, but perhaps much glory.*

"You can smell shame?"

A shrug. A nod.

"And for you is it not also a rescue mission?"

Perhaps.

"What do you mean? The doctor told me when you all first arrived that some had indicated that they wanted to go back to Arla. But I'm sure that was just the shock of it all, of not knowing what might happen next."

I do not speak for the others. I did not even know any of them. A couple were known to me from the training rooms years later when I went back to them. I had not gotten to that in my reports. Also, I am sorry I have no new report for you today yet.

"Do not apologize. This is to be done at the pace you are comfortable with."

Arcana looked at him, his flowing hair deepening the shadows on his face. Finally, he wrote. *My comfort is to please you.*

"That is not necessary. I meant—" He stopped. Arcana was composing again.

Are you not the most powerful man on this ship?

Mordecai said, "What do you mean by power? Strength? I'm sure there are others who are physically stronger."

I mean you tell them all what to do. And they do it.

"I am the captain of this ship, yes."

I saw that instantly the moment I boarded your beautiful ship. The way you command and control and order things. Your ability amazes me. So I will say again, my comfort is to please you.

He thought about that for a moment. He remembered the part of the more recent report where Arcana had quickly learned to adapt to survive, and that meant forgetting his past life and embracing the new. He gave in to pleasure and fell in love when no alternatives were in sight. His pleasure and idea of safety was programmed to respond to strength, authority. A heat at this realization swept through him. Unnerved him. "Pleasing me is an odd way to say you will obey the rules."

I did not say I would obey rules. I said I would please you for my own comfort, and that means abiding by your rules. That is my only wish.

Frowning, Mordecai said, "So you are not concerned with ship's rules?"

Arcana shrugged. He wrote, *No, I am concerned with your rules. Whatever might the ship's rules mean for me?*

"Good question. The rules of this ship are there for the efficiency and safety of its livelihood and its crew."

Arcana nodded, then wrote, *What if the ship must survive but can only do so by breaking the rules?*

"There are protocols in place for that. And human judgment."

One human. The captain. You are that deciding force.

"Yes."

Thus, my comfort depends upon you. I would do all to please you.

More heat at this statement. Mordecai suppressed his shame, not wanting it to show in a darkening of his cheeks. "It's not necessary to do anything to please me, Arcana. I have given a promise to care for any refugees on this ship unconditionally."

If I may ask another question.

"Of course."

Why did you become captain?

The new question distracted his shame. Good. Mordecai was pleased that Arcana had questions. "My father worked in a rocket yard. I admired the ships. I always wanted to command a great star vessel."

Why?

"It seemed like an amazing job, an opportunity."

All right. I understand. You do not wish to answer my question.

"I did answer." He cocked his head, confused.

An opportunity for an amazing job could be gained in many ways and through many choices. You chose command of a great starship. Do you like it?

"Yes."

Why?

"It is like an encapsulated world that runs on a schedule that I can feel a part of, and control."

Ah. You like the control. So do I. You see?

Mordecai shook his head. "Not quite." He felt his brows narrow.

I like control in the way where I know what to expect, at will, through my response to a life of pleasure, of ecstasy. To receive that from a person of power, a person I desire-- There is nothing like it.

Mordecai swallowed hard. He blurted the first question he could think of. "It was Blaek whom you relied on. You were, your report said, in love?"

Oh yes. Very much.

"So you are not happy away from him."

Happy? My comfort and contentment for an unknown future are gone. Therefore, happiness is a state I do not know.

Mordecai felt something in his chest plummet.

"So if you could, would you want to return to Arla?" Now the question he'd really wondered about was out in the open.

Arcana's hands froze on the pad. Mordecai watched his fingers, waited for him to compose. After a few moments he saw drops fall onto the beautiful hands, clear and glistening. Tears.

"Arcana, I am sorry if that upsets you."

He typed. *My being is pure in its ecstasy and torment. I would not wish otherwise.* Arcana looked up, a small smile lighting behind his tears.

Mordecai fought the urge to reach out and press his fingers to those tears, touch that open face. His breath caught. "I do not think I understand you."

Not even from my reports?

Mordecai shook his head. "Would you really want to go back?"

If there is nothing more for me among humans, maybe. But there is nothing more for me on Arla anymore, either. Blaek was in the process of selling me.

"What?" This was brand new news.

There is much more of my report I need to write for you. You only have part of my story so far.

Though slavery in any manner was abhorrent to Mordecai, he did know after reading what he had of Arcana's experiences that this was no small matter. He could not help himself from saying, "I'm sorry. That must have been a terrible feeling for you."

Arcana shrugged. He typed very slowly. *I'm fine.*

He did not have to speak for Mordecai to hear the hesitation in his communication.

"I don't think it would be easy for you."

Arcana blinked and gave a little smile. *I had not gotten to the part of my report where the Arlai grow stale with sameness. I lived with Blaek for seven years. He brought several more slaves into his home during that period. He favored me for maybe five years. After that, I was well cared for, given the pain and the pleasure to be sure, never threatened with being sold as others were, but no longer Blaek's focus. I focused. I am human in that way. That part of me did not leave. I loved Blaek. I still do. But he spent a lot more time at work, sometimes days and nights both. He moved on. Maybe, so shall I?*

Mordecai wanted to tell him how sorry he was again, but held back, unsure. He said, "I know you will move on from this. In the best of ways."

Do you, indeed?

"Of course."

How do you know this?

"I don't actually know. I hope."

Arcana let out a quick puff of air.

Hope was one of the things I learned to do away with during my first days as a captive. I am better for it, too.

"I don't know if a person is better without hope, though."

Well, how could I ever hope for anything better? Do you understand that I do miss Blaek? He drank my pain and my pleasure, devoured me with it and into it. They are the Great

Devourers, the Arlai. So wonderful and pure and devout in their need. I gave in to that need and have become more for it. He fostered my fears, made me pure. I miss that predator who found his prey in me.

"That is," Mordecai paused, "strange to me. I cannot say I completely understand, but I am listening."

The concept of predator and prey is strange to you?

"In terms of discussing humans outside of crime, yes."

That is a surprise. For humans are great predators. And great prey alike. The Arlai were careful to sniff out their stolen ones and reject those with a high, predatory scent. But sometimes they made errors. Those humans went to the breeding farms, I am told. Or perhaps they simply did not survive. The Arlai were tight-lipped about human deaths. They appeared to do all they could to prevent death, actually.

Frowning, Mordecai read the words Arcana wrote twice. "You say they rejected those with a high, predatory scent?"

Yes. As best they could.

"I was almost taken once." Mordecai surprised himself at the admission. His voice came out soft but fast, as if he had no control.

Almost? It is my opinion that if you were not taken, it was because you were not easy prey and they let you go.

Mordecai had known there was a reason he wasn't taken, but never had an answer. The fact that the Arlai abductors had let him escape when his friends had been taken had given him a certain amount of guilt as well.

"But none of you, my friends who were taken included, were easy prey."

No. The training is not easy.

"But by your reasoning, you were taken, not rejected, because you were weak. That is not a comforting thought."

I did not say weak. If I were weak, would I have survived seven years of enslavement that involved daily pain and torture?

It was a true statement. To endure that took strength, no matter that it rewarded him with pleasure in the end.

"I did not mean to imply you were weak. Of course you are a survivor. That takes great fortitude."

I agree.

"So there must be another reason I was rejected other than not being easy prey."

All of us are fighters in various ways. But some will never be able to be devoured and find the purity in that. The Arlai cannot take their pleasure from them.

Mordecai was not sure if he should feel insulted or vindicated. To stem his nerves and discomfort, he put out his hands and shrugged. "I honestly do not understand, but I want to listen to more of your story and try."

Arcana nodded. *This is why I said it is my comfort to please you. Because you do try. You do care.*

"I very much care about your welfare and that of the other rescued men."

Thank you.

"And on that note, I am not sure how to put this, but I am concerned that your friends—or, rather, fellow slaves—could be being taken advantage of on this ship. I'm doing my best to contain it."

Their conditioning is sufficient to direct their choices.

"What does that mean?"

The Arlai made us strong. We could not say "no" to them. But with others we have no such conditioning. The others are not being taken advantage of, as you state it. If your crew and the rescued slaves mingle, it is not through coercion on the part of your crew. The slaves, however, I cannot speak for. We learned coercion from masters of the craft. It might be that it is your men who are being taken advantage of.

"Are you saying my men are the ones being coerced?"

Arcana raised his eyebrows in comment, but otherwise did not type.

Mordecai sighed. "I am not sure you understand that certain social behaviors can be the result of trauma. So I would like a rule in place that my men not mingle with yours for at least two weeks. Our ship's doctor is simply being cautious, as am I. We would not see harm come to you or the others."

Now Arcana typed. *Thank you for the sentiment, but the question really is, what does an individual want, and if that is being kept from them by a narrow belief or law, is that not also doing harm?*

Slightly appalled, Mordecai said, "We do not always get what we want, now, do we?"

In truth, he did not wish to address that the medical ban on the slaves was anything short of the right thing to do. He'd made his decision and was standing by it.

Arcana typed. *I understand. We do not always get what we want. But we are all taught to try to earn it.*

Mordecai gave a small smile. "Maybe there is a little hope left in you to say that."

It is less about hope, more about a means for survival.

"Agreed." He could not think of another time he'd had a more riveting conversation with anyone in his life. Being in Arcana's presence made him hot, then cold. His curiosity kept manifesting in two ways: His mind would race, brimming with questions. And his body would come alive with arousal.

The two responses seemed inappropriate when combined together.

Uncomfortable again, Mordecai stood, letting out a sigh. He needed time to think, to control himself. He needed to leave.

"If I think of more questions for you, I will chime you."

I will have another report for you soon.

"Thank you. But only if you wish. Otherwise, official questions for you about Arla and the Arlai will be forwarded from the xenobiology department."

Arcana looked up at him, a faint smile filling his smooth cheeks. He tilted his head. *Yes, but do you yourself wish for more reports? I do wish to please you.*

He noted with annoyance that now his cheeks began to heat. "Yes, you said that before. But in truth, I do not require them." He could feel his heart pound at his own words. How he wanted them. Yes. But his proclivity for doing right, and for honesty, got in his way.

I did not ask if you require them.

Mordecai blinked hard at that.

Arcana typed nothing more. Head bowed, he stared at his hands.

An overwhelming sadness seemed to walk into the room.

Mordecai stood frozen for a moment, staring at him, wondering at him, confounded by the beauty of him, the intelligence, and the situation. Finally, he turned before his already strong discomfort could get any worse, and left the room.

The corridor air felt instantly cooler than Arcana's quarters. The whiteness of the ship's day-lit bulkheads stung his eyes for a moment. He had not realized how hot it was in there. He breathed in deeply, squared his shoulders, and walked briskly down the hall toward the bridge.

Chapter Seven

He was restless. His mind would not focus on the daily tasks at hand, his normal work.

He told himself all humans were fascinated at some point by the morbid, the profane. He was no different, and that was why his mind could not stop replaying the images conjured from Arcana's reports.

He jogged the short track in the gym between his shifts. During shifts, he immersed himself in work. Or tried. But all he really saw, all day and in his dreams, was that lithe, firm body in the skinsuit, the damp, golden eyes, the shining hair like a banner across Arcana's face as if to hide more and more beauty, the purity of his experience and his now-alien soul, the glow.

Mordecai had never seen such a glow, not even on lovers, or *his* lovers. And never in his own mirror.

He'd had three short relationships. He had thought love was loyalty and commitment, a feeling of trust and even lust. He never knew love might be a spell, a transformative entity unto itself.

But when he thought of Arcana and re-read the reports over and over and felt it all as if he were actually there, he knew that spell of real love had eluded him his whole life. He'd been held back. Never completely open. His feelings of never really feeling safe enough.

Arcana had had horror, but through that, he had found-- something. Mordecai knew he never had. He had been aloof even in his lusts, his anger at himself for feeling such a lack of control, for being so compulsive he could never just bask in another's presence, or even think of feeling "at one" with them as romances would have people believe.

Days passed.

He deliberately went out of his way to not see Arcana. If he could control his obsession—hell, his attraction—which he was sure was all wrong and happening for all the wrong reasons, he was sure it would abate.

But even after three days, all he saw was Arcana in his mind. He would find himself wondering at that man's beauty, his calmness, his insight. Everywhere, even on the plain, white bulkheads humming with the power-soul of the ship, walls that protected the humans from the cold vacuum of space, Mordecai saw cages. The stars exploded against his retinas when he gazed out portholes, untouchable. The gym was a world of slickness and shining bodies of sweat trapped with a need to burn, to get their energy from inside to the outside. The showers he took were waterfalls of cascading diamonds that hurt his eyes. His self-inflicted orgasms longed to take him to depths of meaning like wordless moments of awe when one grasped the meaning of it all only to stumble within mere language to describe that brink. And yet something always held back. It could not decipher, let alone abate, his longing.

What was going on?

He slept in a kind of lethargic state, not deeply, and saw repeated scenes of ugly Arlai with their hard, metallic-sheened bodies, frightened boys (all far too young for him to be having dreams of), and Arcana smiling through his tears, talking about love. He dreamed of the cage where Blaek had put Arcana sometimes, naked and cold. He saw images of alien sex behind his eyes all the time, large Arlai cocks penetrating humans.

Half the rescued men, according to Dr. Teason, had shyly asked if they might return some day to Arla.

Arcana had not. Yet.

On the fourth night of his restlessness, Mordecai saw a new report in his computer's inbox. He had thought maybe Arcana had decided to stop writing them.

He felt his body grow immediately hot. His skin prickled. He was hard all over, tense, yes, and aroused just at the sight of it waiting to be read. Just at the anticipation.

He needed to get control!

Glancing at the top of the report, he read:

Dearest Captain Mordecai:

Though you told me you require no more reports, I sensed you might want more. If I am wrong, then you do not have to read this. You know my story is not yet finished. I hope you will read it. You can tell yourself I wrote this one for myself. And for the official medical files as well. But in reality, I wrote it for you.

I make no apology for the explicit language or the subject matter.

Already that honeyed smile was flashing in Mordecai's mind, that countenance Arcana had of pride, not victimhood, and those beautiful tears against such soft cheeks and accepting smiles.

He was fully hard before he read the first word.

Love, for the Arlai, is like a rare, many-faceted jewel. You might wish to possess it and keep it in a safe for a thousand years, or you might get tired of it and sell it after you have enjoyed its boon and artistry for awhile.

It is not love as humans define it, but it is greatly satisfying for them.

Arla is home to over ten million Arlai. Despite all the raids over thirty some-odd years on Earth colonies, we slaves still made up a minor part of one percent of that population. There were only a few thousand of us, some human children born on Arla still being raised on the breeding farms, born from the few girl-children they took, and the rest of us taken from our human families over the years. We were rare jewels. And quite valuable.

I discovered after a few years that only the wealthiest of Arlai had human slaves. If you were poor, and lucky enough to know wealthy families, slaves could be loaned, shared or even co-owned.

My Arlai, Blaek, was one of the wealthy. He did not need his job. He desired his job. He trained humans in the Punishment Room because he was good at it, because he loved it. It was his own artistry, to train the slaves. And he excelled at it.

I found out he had had two other boys before me. He sold them after a short while, preferring new human blood, the virgins, and the training rooms.

I learned all of this in detail as I continued to live with him and serve him. I have told you about my jealousy at first. I knew he liked the new recruits. I knew that the more I was broken in by him, the more the novelty might wear off.

I worked hard to attract him. I deliberately fought him at times, just to allow the punishments, the whippings. I learned to moan in pain when he took me as if it were my first time, all the while enjoying him, craving him more and more.

There is an addictive sense that human prey and Arlai masters share that cannot be put into words. Perhaps I can simplify and state my Arlai was my drug. I was addicted to his desire of me.

The worse the punishment he threatened me with, the more I would disobey just to endure that punishment, no matter what, so I could have my way with him. You may think we human slaves on Arlai were all cowed and broken and mad. Maybe some of us were. But from my observations, we were addicted to our masters, and we knew what we wanted. We would do anything to get it.

Conditioning. Programming. Sure all of that came into play. We did tricks for pleasure. We were trained, captive sideshow freaks, whores who demanded sex like drug addicts, naked, willing and submissive.

But we were also masters at manipulation. At the end of years of training and being mastered and learning about Arlai love, I came to ask myself who had the real upper hand here?

We were precious to our masters. Any deaths of slaves appeared to be only accidents during the kidnappings or training, or mis-diagnosed health issues.

Knowing that, we all grew to learn we could have whatever we wanted if we just knew our place, the correct behaviors, and rode the pain and pleasure like the most exhilarating journey ever.

And it was. Exhilarating, I mean.

Do not think less of me. Not that it really matters. But I want you to be fair with me. I deserve that. Fairness, not judgment. If anything, I ask it for all of us you rescued. Because our mental health depends upon it. Upon you. You show the others the way. You are the captain. They follow you. They obey you. So to do right by us, you must understand us.

I know some of the others have said they want to return to Arla. I believe they should be able to do so, but at the right time, of course, and we will all look to you to judge that time.

For myself, I know I never said I wanted to go back. And I never said I didn't.

I will tell you now. I do not.

Perhaps this next part of my report will help you understand why.

Blaek and I lived our routine of torture and pleasure for a long time. The Arla year is longer than human years, but only by a month or so. After about two years, Blaek, who had been training new boys all along, and would tolerate no jealousy from me about it whatsoever, brought one of them home.

I was on the cusp of eighteen when I was taken. I am twenty-five now. When the new boy came home, I was well into my twentieth Earth year.

The new one was exactly my age.

I remember the day like it was yesterday. Blaek had been coming home later and later, and more often punishing me without reward, and I was desperate to fix the situation.

That day it was earlier when he arrived, the sky still red before night, the birds chattering and not yet gone to bed, the scent of the grasses over the hot fields still blowing into the open windows of the big house. Night would bring its usual cold and I was just setting the wood for a fire for later, when Blaek came in with "the kid".

70

I hated him on sight. Blond, blue-eyed, pink-cheeked. Pert buttocks and a rosy cock that was, I later saw, always hard. Always. I wanted to hit him. He was weeping so beautifully when Blaek shoved him through the door. He stumbled. On purpose, of course, and looked up adoringly at Blaek.

I could taste my own sour emotions, as if my whole body chemistry changed. I rolled my eyes.

Blaek looked at me. He could smell me from the doorway. He knew my demon. Jealousy.

I expected to be hanged by my ankles from the ceiling beams. Or sent to the cage for a day and night without food or blankets. Or to be whipped soundly all over my body. The thought was already making me hard, the drama I would endure, the pity and comfort I would claim as my own.

Blaek did none of that. He knew what would make me suffer more.

He chained me to the foot of his bed, legs apart, ankles attached to the bottom of the frame, hands together in front. If I tried to move I would fall onto the bed pulling my leg muscles painfully, or fall back on the hard floor, legs wide apart, making a spectacle. I had to stand there, legs out, and face the whole bed.

Blaek took the kid to the bed and trussed him up, wrapping chains about him until his ass was in the air and his hands were high above him. He whipped him nicely and made me watch. When the kid was covered with welts, silently sobbing, he took him from the chains and into his arms and rocked him.

My fury raged. I tried to scream, to yell, but only air escaped my throat.

Blaek watched my silent suffering, and made love to the boy right in front of me, ordering me not to look away. "You will not eat for a week. You will not have orgasms for a month," he threatened me.

He was tender and gentle to the strange boy after the whipping, and the kid had a bigger cock than I did, and wiggled his pert bottom just right. Blaek showed extreme pleasure at entering him, telling the boy he was tighter than any he'd ever had, literally cooing over him. The kid shot his seed like a pro, squirming and coming, a regular little star who could manifest tears and a smirk at the same time. It was so unfair. I was really in love with Blaek. All the kid was doing was faking it.

Blaek came inside him with a yell and I shut my eyes, only opening them when I felt his hand impact my jaw with a heavy smack. His cock was still spurting as he hit me, even though he'd withdrawn from the kid's opening. He turned away from me and let the kid suck him and kept coming. Arlai are like that when they have a new one, insatiable.

Furious, I jerked at my chains and fell back.

Blaek yanked me up and chained me to the toilet in the bathroom, forcing me to watch him bathe the kid, and pleasure him with his mouth. The kid cuddled up to him so sweet, then looked at me over Blaek's side with a glare, as if he'd already bettered me, and I'd better watch out.

Blaek took me from the bathroom, admonishing me. "You stink. That is not the way to greet your brother, is it?"

I made hand signals to communicate: **He is not my brother.**

For that I was taken up into his arms and thrown over his hard shoulder. Blaek spanked me hard on the ass. Much as I had wanted the attention, finally, my cock remained flaccid. He did not like that at all. He took me to the outside cage and left me there in the freezing night.

The next morning, when he came to me, I would not respond to him.

I pouted for two days. I was whipped and hanged upside-down, and forbidden any pleasure. I didn't care.

But I soon learned something. My flaccid cock and jealous scent got me attention. The kid was mad whenever I got punished. I was denied any reward, but I did have my master's focus on me. At least for those times.

The worst was to come, however. I didn't know what Blaek had in store for me when, after several days of punishment, he took me to the shower and gently washed me. I thought maybe he'd finally sent the kid away. He was nowhere to be seen.

When Blaek took me to his bed, I clung to him like the old times when I was falling in love with him. I smiled up at him. But he *ignored my expression, turned me over roughly, ordered me onto my knees, and secured me in that position with the hard chains.*

I didn't mind. If he wanted me that way, I would like it.

But then I heard a noise from behind. I could not turn my head far enough to see, but I heard soft footfalls, and I heard Blaek say, "Brother to brother. I would see you take him."

I stiffened. All my insides tightened. I didn't care if this pleasured Blaek. When I felt the kid's hands on me slicking me up, I tried to get away. I bucked but could barely move. I opened my mouth but no sound came.

When I felt that human cock, the burn and the pain were worse than any Arlai rape. I did not want this boy. He disgusted me. But he didn't notice, or care, and he entered me quite willingly, his hands gripping my hips until his nails dug in. He fucked me fast. He was hot, stiff and eager. I hated him more for that.

"Isn't he pretty?" Blaek asked. I did not know if he was referring to me or the wretched blond who put his hands on me, his cock in me.

I did not cry. My tears were not for misery. My rage was for my misery. It took hold of me like a white fog and did not let go.

I slumped afterward, feeling the kid's liquid all over my back, and listening to Blaek commend him, praise him.

Blaek took my lack of movement as defeat. He unchained me without comment, then pulled me up by one arm and made me face my rapist. He failed to read my body language, my scent, my rage. In that moment, he was satisfied that his new boy had taken the old boy and all was well.

When Blaek let go of my arm and started to turn, I pounced on the kid and began to beat his face and neck with my fists. The kid was so surprised he went over backwards, falling onto his back.

I raged into him, but not for long. My Arlai pulled me up by my hair, then one arm, and held me out from his body as I kicked and flailed.

No punishment was strong enough to contain my rage. Blaek kept me outside in the cage for many days. When he thought I had made peace, he brought me in, and set me at my chair for a meal. I was starving. I ate voraciously. The kid was seated beside me and I could tell he was trying not to smirk. Blaek watched us.

I finished and Blaek ordered me up to clean. I took my dish to the sink and began to clean it. When I came around to the kid, I leaned in to take his empty dish, watching Blaek's expression of approval as I did so. I picked up the plate and slammed it into the kid's face.

Blaek had me in his grip in moments. The kid was hunched over, blood everywhere.

When Blaek pulled me close, I hit him with my fists over and over.

He said to me, my blows falling on hard flesh that seemed never to feel pain, "Do not doubt that I will send you back to the farm and the punishment room if you keep this up."

I stopped punching him and shrugged.

I wanted to be sold on the auction block. I did not want Blaek anymore.

This went on for weeks. Blaek kept threatening to send me away. I kept up my behavior, hoping he would do just that.

The kid smirked and smiled at me whenever Blaek wasn't looking. But one day Blaek caught him making faces at me and sent him, not me, to the cage.

He took me into his bedroom, sat me on the bed facing him, and spoke to me in a way I had not heard for weeks.

"This is not a competition," he began.

I shook my head in disagreement.

"You are my beautiful dark jewel," he said. "He is the light that shines upon that jewel. That is my hope. You shall complement each other, complete each other. That is all I wish."

I shook my head no again.

"You do not know my love," Blaek said.

I questioned him with my eyebrows.

"You do not know that it is boundless. I can love you and him and still have more to give. It takes nothing from you."

Never had he spoken to me this way before. I began to sob. He held me and did not hit me that time. He licked my tears as they fell and seemed surprised at their taste. His cock hardened. He licked me all over. He sucked me to hardness. He ignored his own arousal and took mine into his mouth, all the release, the tears, the spill from my cock, and then rocked me to sleep, his webbing surrounding me. He slept with me the entire night.

This time the kid was in the cage.

After that, I worked hard to ignore the kid. But sometimes it was hard. Blaek would hold both us in his lap at once, one on each arm, and play with us. It gave him extreme gratification to have two of us, but I didn't care.

Blaek never told me the kid's name, or said it out loud in my presence, and the kid never signed it to me. Honestly, though we both inhabited the space in the arms of our master, we did not ever come to care for each other.

One day, maybe a year and a half later, the kid was sent away. I was happy again for some time. But new ones came, and there was nothing I could do about it. Luckily, all were temporary, never staying for more than a few days.

Seven years I lived on Arla with Blaek. After about five years, our passion became even more routine, a habit. The others that came and went quickened him, I understood that. Strangely, it quickened me for him through my jealousy for a time. I learned that he needed more than I could give. I didn't have to like it. It was just the way of Blaek. The stimulus of other boys brought him new wonder and great release. He could not get enough. We had rekindlings of our passion with each boy. But he never ordered one to rape me again. Once in awhile my rage ignited. But by then Blaek knew all too well how to handle me.

I only came to like one of the boys a little bit. Dusty they called him. He was nineteen and I twenty-two at that time. He was a little guy. I liked him because when I hit him the first time, he clung to me as if I were the master, all hard and wanting. It made me feel quite powerful. We played around with each other. I loved pinching him until he cried, then sucking his little perky cock until he spurted down my throat. When Blaek would catch us doing that, we were severely punished. But we didn't stop.

I had thought maybe Blaek would like to see us together, getting along, especially after the kid, but I never caught him watching.

At least I wasn't jealous for once!

Dusty stayed for the most amount of time of any of them. Just under two years. I thought because I finally liked one of the boys, that would mean he would stay longer. But that was not to be. I always wondered if I had turned the tables, if Blaek was now the jealous one, not I.

A tiny part of me was sorry to see Dusty go.

Time changes people. Seven years I had been with Blaek when your people from **Prince Fair** *came.*

In those last years, I had become an Arlai. I was Arcana; nothing was left of the boy who had been taken at seventeen.

Blaek knew it. I kept thinking he would finally take me to the auction block, sell me. I was not what he craved any longer. Instead, he began to take me with him to work. I assisted him in training. It is true that training slaves is an art.

I became an Arlai in that way, too. I became my own version of a Devourer, finding it easy to give pain and delight so the new ones could achieve the purity I'd found. But my own purity was fading. And I longed for it to return.

But now... now I feel new again, as if I have ascended to another level. It feels good to be here on your ship under your command.

Do you understand what I am saying?

Do you know now why I do not wish to return like some of my brothers?

It is over for me now. All of it. Blaek. My love for him that I can never have again. That was all happening to me before you came. This change. Strangely, everything I have learned from the Arlai has prepared me for the choices I wish to make for my future path,

As a final statement to you, Captain, I would like to say that your memos to the crew and guests aboard **Prince Fair** *in your attempt to regulate social, sexual and other private behaviors may come from your idea of doing what's right and ethical. But that, sir, is your idea and not necessarily shared by others. It is commendable* *that you wish for the full health of the slaves you rescued to be restored to them, but each one, as an adult, must be allowed to make his own decision. Perhaps they wish to be acclimated back into your ship's culture of protocols and proper decorum. Or perhaps they wish to sell their bodies to the highest bidder and be forever pampered by rough, rich men who seek to exploit them. Either way, it is not your decision.*

*

That night, Mordecai got maybe one hour of sleep.

Chapter Eight

"I look human, don't I?" Arcana said. "On the outside."
He was smiling when Mordecai entered his quarters.

Mordecai had never heard his voice before. It came on
the air like a low, fluid wind, sounding partially lost and
partially found.

"I see you've found your voice."

Mordecai felt he needed to see Arcana again, but had
been avoiding Arcana until that last report. After reading it
multiple times, he realized he had been a fool. He could
control himself. He'd spent a lifetime doing so. What did he
have to be afraid of?

Arcana was seated by a window viewscreen, gazing at
the rushing stars. He wore a red skinsuit. His golden coloring
was flamboyant against the hue of the material. A large ficus
grew by the window in a planter built into the bulkhead. The
green leaves seemed to reach out and brush Arcana's bright,
brown hair but, in reality, it was Arcana who subtly tilted his
head.

The man looked up at Mordecai, his eyes a deep amber,
brighter than even the starry window. This man, Mordecai
knew, lived in the very depths of the pure elixir of life itself.
Pleasure, pain, rapture. Utter openness. No denial.

Mordecai cleared his throat. "I read your report, of
course."

"Do you need more?" came the soft voice again. It was
beautiful, like listening to new music.

Mordecai nodded, then shook his head. But what he
really wanted to do was say over and over, *Yes. Yes.*

What are you doing to me? He wanted to ask. Instead, he
said, "The men who want to return to Arla? What am I to do?
I cannot, in good conscience, allow them to go back."

"It is your ship." Arcana smiled. "You do not have to allow them anything."

That beautiful voice. How could the Arlai have ever wanted to take it away? It was making him lose his focus. "That's not what I meant."

"It is. You have a code you live by. Ethics, too. It is difficult not to put that onto others ostensibly for their own good." For not speaking Standard in years, Arcana had a wonderful memory of the language now.

"The Arlai did that to you, put their own ethics onto you, but through horror, torture."

"And pleasure," Arcana added.

"But they did it by force. I am not forcing anything onto anyone. I simply find it abhorrent to return anyone to a situation of terror and abuse."

"My last report. What did you think?"

Mordecai felt heat rise to his face. "What did I think?" He stumbled over the words.

"Do you understand things better because of it?"

"It was quite---uh, informative."

"Good."

"Do you really think of yourself as an Arlai now?"

"I went through a life-changing experience. It is a permanent part of me now. Perhaps I do not have the sense of smell they do, but it is enhanced. As is every other sense I possess. Perhaps I do not have their strength of appetite, or their jaded longevity, but I do understand their uninhibited need, and how a reveal of that, and its shameless release, has given them a long peace for millennia. There is no violence or war on their world."

"Whippings are not violence?" Mordecai argued. "And kidnapping and rape and castration and mutilation?"

"No war or violence between them, between each other. No violent outbursts. That is what I mean. We slaves have the power to gift them that. Unashamed."

Mordecai set aside his outrage, his pre-conceptions, and simply considered Arcana's words themselves. "Would you want to go back to that?"

"You read my report. I told you I do not wish to return."

"But you condone it for others because of some purity of bliss you achieved?"

Arcana's eyes filled. "No."

Mordecai slumped at the one-word response. He was no mental health expert, but it did seem perhaps normal the Arcana was conflicted. He moved to the bench where Arcana was perched, and sat beside him. He lowered his head and spoke. "They are monsters."

Arcana did not slump. He sat straight, regal. "Yes. And I met them and survived. And fell in love. And survived even that, great love, which, stronger than fear and pain, was my greatest lesson."

"I don't know how to respond to that."

Out the corner of his eye, he could see Arcana, all in red, like an unshakeable work of art, unbent before him. Open. Unapologetic. Only twenty-five years old but with the calm bearing of the greatest of spiritual masters.

"When you don't know how to respond, you do not have to say anything at all. It is all right," Arcana said.

"Must one go through a fire to understand it is hot?"

"Are you referring to the pain I endured and was purified by, or the pleasure?"

"Both, I suppose. But mostly the pain. Why go through it?"

"Some must. You must know what it is like to accomplish a mission, to master a plan. To feel in control. All of that really is an illusion, but to feel that? There is nothing better. To let go, however, is total and pure ecstasy, acceptance. Only then can you know the truth. What control means. What it does. How it sets you up to finally, willingly to let go. Pain is an instigator for that. So is pleasure. The Arlai

80

drink both and enjoy both equally, thus they programmed us for both experiences. The pain was harder, of course, but when one craves pleasure, one will go through fire to get it."

"Maybe. Sometimes."

Mordecai's body gave a quick jerk when he felt the soft hand against his own on the bench. The warmth there, heart-stopping in its subtle simplicity, like a lover's caress. Spikes of pleasure coursed through his body at that touch. He did not want to draw away. But his throat formed the word. "No."

So soft and warm, that touch. Gentle. Quiet. Safe, but not quite.

He looked up, keeping his hand still. Arcana did not move. The heat between them grew.

Slowly, he turned his head. Arcana's eyes swam—always those damned sweet tears—reflecting starlight.

"Everything about you says yes. From day one." That dulcet voice.

A thrill shifted through him, then panicked him. He wanted Arcana. Arcana wanted him. Had this been a seduction all along? Of course it had, with the reports… everything.

And yet this man was a victim of rape, abuse. How could Mordecai believe Arcana's mind was clear about this and not so broken he was incapable of free choice?

Frowning. "No." Still, he did not pull back his hand. Mordecai lifted his head. Their gazes met. Sharp. Gentle. Determined. Open.

"Why?" Arcana's voice whispered over him.

"Because it would be wrong." He hesitated on that last word. Unsure.

"Would it?" Arcana's face seemed to grow bigger. Mordecai blinked. The younger man came closer. Slow, oh so slow, barely noticeable, until Mordecai could feel Arcana's breath, smell the sweetness, even the salt of his tears. He wondered what it would be like to touch those lips with his own. To feel the fullness press to his mouth, the opening of that pink mouth, the giving way of his own mouth, the shared moisture and breath.

Startled at his own fantasy, he glanced away and pulled his hand back, standing abruptly. "It would," he finally said.

Without looking back, he turned and left the room.

Striding through the corridor, everything a blur, he kept thinking, *It isn't what he wants anyway. Not that gentle touch. He wants whippings. Force arouses him. I like control, yes. But I cannot give him that. He said it himself. He is not human. He is scarred by trauma. Not responsible. I would be taking advantage. I would only open myself to face loss.*

When he got to his quarters, he leaned against the closed door to catch his breath, his entire body throbbing with a mixture of horror and regret.

*

After that meeting, he tried again to avoid Arcana. He spoke to no one about him, not even Dr. Teason. But he could not rid his mind of his fantasies. And he could not avoid Arcana forever.

Over the next few days he brushed by him in the corridor, or saw him on the rec deck, or wandering by the stores. Every time he saw him, his heart rate increased, his skin grew fevered.

He had read all the reports again.

His guilt at what he wanted, and what was his reality as captain of a ship overseeing the safety of all aboard, grew. He was human. Arcana was no longer. The impossibility of anything between them stretched long and wide, deeper than the distances between planets.

Besides, there was his own two-week ban. The memos to his ship's complement. Crew could not mingle with Arlai slaves.

82

He received daily medical reports on the progress of therapy, or refusal of therapy, for all nine rescued men. Arcana was one who refused therapy, but his physical health was at one hundred percent now. Reports on the others indicated four of the men were having trouble sleeping and eating, and were suffering from depression. It was interesting to note that half of the eight slaves wanted to be returned and the other half did not. Four wanted to be left alone, like Arcana. Two had indicated, on their second day after being rescued, they wished to go back to Arla, but had not made any requests since then. Two more made subsequent requests to be returned. Only one man still was not speaking. All were now in good health, aside from the mental tensions.

Reports further stated that any sort of attempted group therapy did not seem to help these men. They did not appear to have normal empathy toward each other, and though they had been together in a line-up when taken, they claimed to be strangers to one another.

Mordecai knew from Arcana's statements that he had participated in training new slaves. He even insinuated he was familiar with a couple of the rescued men. Arcana had an understanding of the situation that went beyond anything Mordecai had ever imagined. He knew Arcana could possibly help the men. He needed to interview him again to ask him about that, but fought seeing him for another couple of days.

*

The rec room had blue bulkheads, soft lighting, and lots of green plants along the edges. The ceiling was a mix of summer sunset colors, rose, lavender, sparkling cerulean. Arcana sat at a holo-console, but he was not involved in what it provided. Instead, he had turned half-way in his seat to face two men whom Mordecai recognized as workers in programming from the upper decks. Mordecai remembered them as M'kir and Duth. He did not know them personally, but he was nothing if not obsessive, and he had memorized all the names of his crew the first day he had taken command of *Prince Fair*.

The men did not notice Mordecai enter. As he approached, he heard one say, in a soft but ugly tone, "You're just a slut, aren't you?"

The second said, "You liked it, alien-fucker."

He quickened his step, hands becoming fists. "Hey!" He felt his right arm come up. The rage that always simmered deep inside him wanted release. He did not intend to actually hit a member of his crew, but Arcana did not know that. As Mordecai's fist threatened the closest crewman, Arcana was there, and his palm impacted with Mordecai's upper arm as if to stop him. Arcana gripped strong, his stance steady and unruffled. The strength surprised Mordecai.

Through gritted teeth, Mordecai said to the two men who were backing away, "You are on report! Get lost!"

Eyes wide, they exited quickly.

He turned to Arcana, who still had his arm in a firm hold. "I was only gesturing. I would never hit a crewmember."

Arcana let go but made no comment.

He noted the man wore a green skin suit today. Yesterday's had been blue. Blue for distance. Green for come ahead? A small smile played at the corners of Arcana's lips. He looked as if he'd just been on the receiving end of victory. A new game. The winner glowing.

"I'm sorry," Mordecai said, lowering his arm. Arcana released him.

"You threaten to attack your crew often?" His tone held no hint of accusation.

"I'll make sure they won't bother you again. And no, I do not attack my crew members or threaten them. This situation simply caught me off-guard."

"There are rumors on this ship, you realize."

Mordecai's eyebrows rose. "What rumors?"

84

"That I'm easy. Is that the word, *easy*? On Skyover we called that sort a tramp. Every planet has its favorite term. Whore. That's the one I also heard on Skyover when someone wanted to insult someone else."

Arcana's words only made Mordecai more incensed. A victim of kidnapping was not to blame. He had almost been one of them, a boy disappeared, vanished from life. "You do not deserve this sort of treatment from them or anyone."

"I do not deserve? What do I deserve, then?" Again, no accusation. His tone had little inflection.

"Humane treatment. Respect." Maybe more. He clamped down on that thought, fighting even now his attraction to this man, to his beauty that comprised not only his physicality but his voice, his stance, his seemingly inner light. He had never expected anyone who had been through what Arcana had to have such a light remain within.

"As everyone else deserves it?" Arcana asked.

"Of course. Including the others who were rescued along with you. They are not all doing quite as well as you, and I came to ask if you might speak to them. I hoped maybe you could help them?"

"So that is why you sought me out?"

A hesitation. "Yes."

"Why me?"

"Because you seem the wiser somehow."

Arcana sighed. "I don't know any of them. Why would they even listen to me?"

"I thought you insinuated you knew a couple of them."

"I don't. I saw a couple of them, yes, in passing. I don't know them."

"I thought they might look to you, the oldest. You have all been through the same ordeal."

"I don't assume that. I loved my master. Maybe some of them did, too, or hated their masters. I can't know. No slave is the same. Treatments are adapted to each one. In general, we all went through similar ordeals. Beyond that, in specifics I can only speak for myself. They will have their own reports to write or not write as they choose."

Mordecai had suspected Arcana would respond this way. He could not help but be disappointed. "I thought, or rather, hoped you would help." He turned toward the door.

"It is not a question of *would* I help them, but *could* I help them," Arcana replied calmly. "I don't think I can."

Mordecai faced him again. "I was only asking."

"I know." A brief sadness tinged the beautiful voice.

Mordecai took a deep breath. The grief in Arcana's tone awakened him. Empathy. A surge of protectiveness. More? Feeling that familiar heat of obsession with this man, his mind urged him to leave. But his body did not want to. What he wanted to do was take him into his arms. Hold onto that mysterious inner candescence. He longed for—what? Just a kiss? A quick fuck? No. Everything. He longed for everything from this man. And more if there was such a thing. The slow burn of it had begun, circling through his arteries and his veins even before he'd walked into the rec room.

Who had he been kidding? In three days, his obsession had not waned. It had only hidden itself.

This couldn't happen.

He looked at the figure in the green skinsuit, narrow-waisted, tall, strong. Beautiful. *Green is not come ahead*, his mind corrected from his earlier thoughts. *Green is for distance.*

He took a deep breath. It took all his will power to head for the door.

"Captain?" came the soothing voice behind him.

He pretended he didn't hear him, and the door slid closed behind him.

Chapter Nine

A new report sat flashing on his screen. No, not a report. A letter.

Dearest Captain Mordecai:

I am writing this because you always leave too soon during our face to face meetings. You have questions but you never get around to asking them all. I have some answers. But I often do not think of them until later, after you have gone.

Our last meeting, I fear, did not go well. Perhaps I should have allowed you to continue to threaten your own man? On Arla, I would not have reacted. But in human company, I am a quick learner. On your ship, it is not the way, officially, for adult humans to strike other adult humans to control them. I mistakenly thought you were about to do that. I should have remembered that as the captain you are taught and required to know what is best.

Please know that my statement is not meant to judge. Or if I do judge, it is in your favor, for I did understand there was honor in your defense of me, but what I did not understand was that it would not revert to violence. For there is a simmering fire inside you that I can see, but I misjudged that.

You stated I deserved respect. You have shown me that. Yes, I noticed.

There are other things I sense about you. I wish to say them, but am not as bold as you may think.

As for my reports, I never really took you to the end of my tale. To my seventh year. Having just turned twenty-five.

I was on my way to the auction block with eight other slaves when your people came and took us. The Arlai your crewmembers attacked was not Blaek. He was the groomsman getting us ready to be sold, then taking us through the city to the auction fair.

So technically, even now, I still belong to Blaek. That should be in the report, for it is the truth.

Also, I fear I was remiss in describing to you Arlai cities as well. I did not see a lot, living in the country, but that last day I can say I should have been impressed moving through one of the major cities of Arla's northern hemisphere, the streets like endless conveyer belts, the buildings like giant gold chess pieces. But I was so angry I did not look around much. I remember scents of florid sweetness, and a peaceful hum of life unlike human cities that are noisy, bustling, tense. Tears rolled down my face, but they were not of sugar anymore. They stung my eyes. It made it hard to see, to be amazed.

I was so angry. All my rage was turned toward Arla. I hated their silences, and their perfection in architecture, routine, torture. I hated all things Arlai in that moment. I hated the city because it wasn't the country. It wasn't rolling fields and yellow sunshine and the familiar coolness of Blaek's large home. I did not want to be taken away again. Not again. I had already lost a home once. Skyover. I could not take it a second time.

I'd lost my purity, the purity Blaek had taught me through pain, through pleasure. The Arlai way, the Arlai's interpretation of love had left me. I'd been rejected. I was empty. I was nothing. All the wisdom I had learned could no longer help me.

Blaek did not love me anymore. And I was to be sold.

I wanted to die.

Your people came upon us. They may say we were docile or that we fought. I don't quite remember. I have not been shown the reports. But I will say that if I did struggle, I only pretended.

I went willingly to your ship. I miss Blaek. But he would not have me anymore. I'd grown. I'd changed. I had learned control so well that nothing I did seemed impulsive for him anymore. Or maybe he never loved me the way I loved him.

I do not want to go back to Arla. And that is why. Not because of pain or enslavement, but only because I lost love, contentment.

I am on a journey to find those again. I am grateful it is far away now from Blaek.

You should know you are a good man. Perhaps you think you are not, but you would be wrong.

That is all.

Arcana

*

Arcana still signed his Arlai name. Strange, for the letter seemed to indicate he was searching on a more human path now. But after reading the reports many times, Mordecai understood Arcana, as an Arlai slave for so many years, could never erase that part of himself. Nor did he appear to want to.

Tyler was the boy who was taken. Arcana was the man who came back.

The last part of the letter only made things harder for Mordecai. Arcana thought Mordecai was a good man. But in all conscience, how could a good man be attracted to, and aroused, by a captive slave's story?

Mordecai did not long for any experience like that for himself. In fact, he was abhorred. Yet, he kept re-reading the reports.

He could not deny the eroticism in them. Yet it felt wrong, even as the dark beauty of Arcana, and the dark horror of his story, followed him into his dreams.

He did not feel like a good man.

*

Mordecai had just finished reading Arcana's letter for the fifth time when his office door chimed. It was late.

He opened the door with the flick of a switch.

Arcana stood in the corridor, backlit by soft white light that enhanced his hands, face, hair and tan-booted feet. This time his skin-suit was white, and it blended with the white bulkheads behind him, though Arcana glowed far brighter with a radiance that seemed almost supernatural.

White for purity? Mordecai's conscience asked. But no, Arcana had said he'd lost that for himself.

"May I come in?" Arcana stated. "It is presumptuous of me to ask at this hour, I know."

"Of course you may come in." Mordecai waved him to a chair.

But Arcana did not sit. Instead, he strode toward a wall of shelves and began to examine the cases and volumes and knickknacks there.

Mordecai watched him, allowing the intrusion. The white skin-suit accentuated the long lines of Arcana's back, the gentle sweep of his buttocks, the firm grace of his thighs. Mordecai's body quickened. He took a breath and held it, silent, waiting.

Arcana picked up a smooth, purple cube. "What is this?"

"An Altairian music-cube."

"Interesting. Blaek had something like this." He lowered his eyes, the thick lashes making shadows on the tops of his cheeks. He turned back toward the shelves where real books in thick, clear cases stood. "Do you read a lot?"

"I do." Mordecai cleared his throat, realizing his voice was rough. He waited impatiently for the man to say why he had come. But he was not really annoyed.

Arcana merely nodded. Then he said, still facing away, "I have never truly been alone my whole life."

"You were very young when you were taken."

"I'm young still," Arcana replied. "That is partially why I am here, to tell you I do not want to be taken back to Skyover. Nor to Earth. And I know Earth is where this ship is headed."

"Where then?"

Arcana shrugged, picking up a small statue of a cloaked figure, and running his fingers over the smooth back of the piece.

"I wanted to also say I am not complaining, but I am not enjoying my quarters. They are stale and lonely. And when I go out, there are many stares. And other things. I can handle myself, of course. But it's annoying."

"I know." Mordecai was still livid over the rec room incident.

"Maybe if I could share quarters with someone--"

Mordecai's heart skipped at the casual statement. "Another of the men from Arla, perhaps?"

"No, I do not like other Arlai slaves. You know this from my reports and from our discussion about me helping, or rather, not helping them."

"I could ask around, see if any crewmembers are willing to share," Mordecai began. One thing at a time. He couldn't fix it all at once. Arcana's new destination. Arcana's loneliness. Arcana's potential, future harassments.

Arcana looked up at him again. Their eyes met. Mordecai's insides went cold, then hot, then cold again. He let out a short sigh.

Arcana said, "Am I really so deplorable?"

"What?"

"You don't like me, I think." The hair fell into one eye as his head tilted, a characteristic Arcana had that was endearing.

Mordecai frowned, almost sputtering. "That is not the case at all!"

Smooth eyebrows rose. A soft beginning of a smile, but not quite there yet, still too sad. "I could stay with you, then. You wouldn't even know I was here. But despite your denial, I am still not sure you like me."

The audacity of the first suggestion shocked Mordecai, and thrilled him. But he was still mulling over the last question. "I do not think you are deplorable! I don't know how you could say such a thing."

"Thank you for that, at least."

Mordecai frowned. His body hoped. His mind rebelled. "But you could not stay here. What would the crew think?"

"The crew think what you tell them to think. You are, after all, the captain." The soft lips curved up a little more. "But I understand. You don't want me here."

"That is not—" he stopped himself.

Arcana gave a small huff. "I would sleep on the floor, of course, be no burden. Perhaps even give you one or two good conversations. But you don't want that. I can see. You are good at being alone. I am not. I have nightmares. I am sometimes afraid of my own thoughts. Everything is new to me now. Different." He turned from the shelves and made his way to the chair in front of Mordecai's desk.

Mordecai watched as Arcana sat and gracefully crossed his legs. A great wave of longing swept over him. The room seemed filled with electricity. He saw blue specks. The air smelled momentarily of the fresh sweets his father would bake on holidays. This inner response was every reason not to share quarters with him.

Mordecai shook his head, realizing what an ass he was making of himself. He wanted Arcana, but it was keeping him from seeing to a basic need for the man. In his early star-faring days, he'd shared cabins before. It was a normal setting. Both for him and others.

"I'm sorry you are having trouble being alone. I understand things are very different for you now." He took a breath. "I've shared quarters with men before. So--"

"You have?" Arcana interrupted.

He nodded.

"May I ask: Friends, or more?"

"Both."

"Men as more?" The golden stare did not waver.

Mordecai held it steady, trying to appear unfazed. "Yes."

"That was perhaps too personal for me to ask."

Mordecai started to respond, then stopped. Trying to form coherent thoughts, he finally said, "You have shared everything personal about yourself. I think I can answer a few questions myself."

"It is too much to expect, I'm aware," Arcana said, his lovely voice soothing Mordecai's thoughts as if without effort. "But you are the only one I really know even a little on this ship. So I came to you."

Of course, Mordecai thought, Arcana should come to him as ship's captain with any problems, questions, suggestions.

Yet all the while his body was turning into a focused inferno. And a whirl of guilt. Would reaching out to him be so very wrong?

Mordecai said, "Very well. I could put you up. You would not have to use the floor. An extra bunk could be brought in. I have the largest personal quarters on the ship on the other side of the entrance alcove. There is ample room."

"I understand I could not live here. Not really. I'd have to leave. Soon. But as I said, I do not want to go to Earth. Not Earth. Nor Skyover."

His mind swam with the unknowns this man now faced. Where would he live? What sort of job would rehab find suited to him?

"One thing at a time. Coming back after seven years away will not be a quick assimilation. We can talk about that. I can help you investigate other alternatives."

"You would do that for me?"

"Of course." But his throat was dry. In truth, he wanted to do more for Arcana than that.

"But you have been standoffish to me. Why are you doing this?"

He frowned. "I have not been standoffish. I've been-- friendly." He moved to lean against his desk, facing the younger man. "Haven't I?"

Arcana let his head bow. He did not answer.

"In truth, if I am cold-seeming, I apologize. You fascinate me. But after your ordeal, I often am unsure what to say, or how to say it."

"I understand awkwardness. Thank you for admitting that, at least. Honesty is the best route. I am new at this, too, being a rescued slave that is."

"It's settled. You can stay here, then." Was this a mistake? He could not allow himself to think it. Arcana seemed so relieved.

"I appreciate it. I promise to be on my best behavior."

Mordecai almost let out a laugh, both amused and mortified at himself, uneasy at Arcana's word choice. Best behavior? In what regard?

"I will order the extra bunk."

Chapter Ten

After their meeting, Arcana did not leave. Ship's evening turned the bulkheads purple and gray. Mordecai ordered the bunk brought in that very hour. Arcana's scant belongings were also retrieved.

Arcana sat at a table in the bedroom and busied himself with his tablet. The doors on either side of the alcove remained open. Mostly Arcana was quiet, and Mordecai found himself not disturbed at all by the presence of him in his personal quarters.

In fact, he liked the company, and his normal evening tensions eased. He had forgotten how nice it was to have another presence in his space. It had been a long time, and with bitter reflection, since Isault had left. He did not miss him at all. But deep inside, he had missed the company of another.

Mordecai concentrated on work. Steeling himself and focusing his mind, he did not allow himself to think about captivity, beauty, desire. For the most part, he succeeded.

Still, once both were readied for sleep in their bunks, yet again he could not sleep. Part of his mind was all too aware of another sleeping in the same room with him, the shushing of the sheets on the other bunk, the soft, smooth breaths. But it wasn't because it was any general presence. It was because it was Arcana. This particular kidnapped boy. This rescued man. This Arlai slave.

Now his steely resolve failed.

The man's beauty distracted him, of course, but also his plight. It was difficult to be honest with himself, but quite simply he was crazily attracted to this man. He'd made great efforts to avoid Arcana in between necessary interviews with the man. Yet now here he was sharing quarters with him.

Bunkmates. Mordecai had behaved in a ridiculous manner. He still was.

After what seemed like hours of tossing and turning, with the object of his disturbance only about eight feet away, he finally drifted off.

*

At first he thought his alarm had wakened him. Then he heard a rasping sound. It sounded like silent sobs.

He sat up. "Arcana?"

"Yes?"

"Are you all right?"

A sigh was the reply. The unwavering voice said, "A nightmare only. Of twisting neverness." His tone seemed nonchalant, yet Mordecai had had dreams like that himself in the past, especially during star-travel slumber, and they were nothing short of disturbing.

"I have had that same dream."

"And I dream of Arla."

The urge to reach out, to help, to speak overwhelmed him. He kept his voice low. "You may not believe you have suffered for the entire seven years of your captivity," he said into the dimness. "You may think that you wanted what happened to you after a certain point. It doesn't change the fact that you were subjugated and sold as a commodity, a thing. How can you not have nightmares? No living being deserves that."

No answer.

"Will you be able to go back to sleep?"

"Maybe. If you talk to me. I'm not using my tears to manipulate, as I learned to do. So please don't think—"

"All right," Mordecai interrupted. "I won't think it." He heard covers moving, saw the silhouette of Arcana in the darkness sitting up.

"But I must be a monster in the eyes of humans," Arcana said softly. "Your men in the rec room were right. They called me alien-fucker. And I did enjoy it. After everything, how can you think I am not some twisted, alien creature? Or trust my motivations in anything? Even now?"

Interesting. Mordecai sat up himself, ever unable to quell his intrigue with this man. "Who can truly trust anyone's motivations? You must know this for a fact even if you can't process it right now. It was Blaek who was the monster."

It was easier, in full darkness, to have a conversation with Arcana. They had not talked like this before, so intimately, at least not in person.

Again, the guilt shot through Mordecai. After everything Arcana had confessed and shown to him in all its vulnerability, why hadn't they talked more? He should have gone and talked to him every day! Any decent human being would have. Mordecai was only now beginning to see he had played his role too hard, along with holding too tight to his precious shame.

In the dark it was easier. Everything was. Even secretly wishing Arcana's motivation for the conversation might be about more than nightmares was easier. A slow flame curled inside his belly. Did he really want to be pushed into doing the very thing his mind had ruled against? Touching Arcana. Wanting Arcana.

Hearing him talk about nightmares, tears, ulterior motives—Mordecai liked it. His impulse for control always at the forefront, letting go was difficult for him. He wanted to get up, move next to Arcana and simply hold him. Hold him?

He took a deep breath. Most definitely, he had been alone for too long.

Now a beautiful man sat in his room in the middle of ship's night.

He scrunched his eyelids tightly together.

Foremost in his mind the explosions of light and desire and even a kind of animal magnetism burned at the very thought.

He remembered back to the day he'd seen him in the stark, dry air of the shuttle bay. That first moment he'd noticed him--yes, even then he'd wanted him.

Arcana.

And there was no longer any point in denying Arcana wanted him in return.

He took another deep breath, the sound loud in the darkness.

Arcana said, "You said you would talk to me."

His eyes opened. Dark on dark again. The room less lonely because of another presence. "Yes. I did. I—I will."

He could almost hear Arcana smile. Saw in his mind the patience of him, even after everything he'd been through, that brilliant glow. He focused, could almost make out Arcana's long, warm shape. Three steps away.

"I have unnerved you, I know," Arcana nearly whispered. "I am not sorry."

Nodding, Mordecai said, "Yes. I admit you have."

"Can I tell you another story?"

The sudden question set him on edge. In a good way. "Yes." Honesty now. Simple, even breaths. He thought back on all the reports, all the words, the feelings, the pain and eroticism of what had been done to this man, and the deeper reaches Arcana had traveled because of it. What would this story be?

"When I first arrived here, "Arcana began, "I was experiencing a lot at once. Still the anger, of course. I wrote of that to you. I wanted Blaek back, what we had before. It was all I ever really knew. But that was gone, and had been gone for two years. That intensity. That richness. But also, I was feeling shock. Here I was back among humans. Real humans, not Arlai slaves. I had been saved from the auction block, and yet I was now standing upon a cold deck with uniformed men

98

surrounding me. It wasn't the pity or judgment from other humans that concerned me. I didn't care about that, but more about trading one confinement for another. One set of rules for different ones. I didn't think about better or worse, I only felt myself begin to anticipate the changes, changes I might not want, and yet again finding myself in a position of little control.

"Out the corner of my eye, I saw you watching me, Captain. Straight and stiff. Your uniform sparkled, perfect, not a stitch out of place. You were a sculpture, molded to represent power and beauty in your own way, your human starship captain way."

Arcana paused.

Mordecai swallowed against a dry throat. Had that been a compliment or not? He wasn't sure.

"I felt calm, then, when I noticed you. My insides were like ash. Not broken wood-flaked ash, but soft and sifting, making its way through my body, a smooth transition, I told myself. But it was a lie. Not everything had burned down yet. Not everything was ash. There was a part of me that wasn't smooth, that craved a sound, an expression from myself. Anything, maybe even something like throwing myself against a wall until I bled. I don't know. I wanted some action. It was indefinable, more than tears might get me. I couldn't yell. I had no voice. And the tears still came. The way I was programmed to cry. The way crying brought me pleasure and the things that might need. It was all I knew. Like a baby."

He paused. Mordecai remained silent, listening. Other than writing reports, this was the most Arcana had ever spoken. Aloud.

"I looked for something to hold onto, to keep me afloat in the new chaos I was thrust into. After seven years, I was adept at seeking the power I craved."

Again, a pause. Then, softly, "I saw you and I knew, then. Recognized it. What I needed. In you."

Before Mordecai could even react, Arcana's words came quicker.

"Later, you met me and asked me to write it all down. So calm I was, and yes, I thought I would write it. All of it. That would be my action. My scream, so to speak. But I would do it without censor. And I would put in all my feelings. All of them, even the dark ones. I hoped my words would take you with them. With me. I used them to seduce you." A little laugh sounded through the space between them.

But Mordecai was not smiling.

"I failed, of course. You are unflappable."

What could he say? The churning inside him was beginning to drown out even his own thoughts. For the first time in—what?—forever?—a warmth began to seep behind his eyes.

"The Arlai are armored on the outside. But you have it inside."

"I don't know what to—" Mordecai stopped. Should he be insulted?

"Shh! I am not finished!"

Mordecai leaned forward, bunching the sheet in his fists.

"It is attractive to me. That armor inside you. And so I wrote my reports far more intimately for you. But you probably did not ever suspect anything else from me, for I am an Arlai slave and cannot help myself, right? But you were attractive to me, and so I wanted to take you down my own path, have you just where I wanted you. But there you are, still three steps away, and thinking about my comfort first, and nothing ever to do with yours. Unflappable."

The sheets gathered at Mordecai's waist. He was shirtless and on his naked skin he could feel the heat of the room increase. The inferno of the other man, of everything he was, had done, had suffered, had dreamed, sent the lightest tendrils, white-hot, licking at his arms, his chest.

Arcana's voice grew even lower. "I have one last thing to try, though. One last attempt I'd like to make."

Eyes wide, Mordecai's thoughts began to spiral. Random. In fragments. He saw hooded figures flying toward him. Isault pushed by Mordecai's own hands and shaking rage, falling hard against a table. Falling. (He'd never hit a crewmember before. And hadn't since.)And the distances of space, how like himself they were, empty but with far glimmerings waiting to be found. He saw Arlai faces from holos, egg-shaped heads, purple faces. And the long line of naked men, some without scrotums, scarred and voiceless in his beloved ship's bay.

What kind of universe was this? What kind of men lived within it?

"No," he finally said aloud, stupid and utterly afraid now. He could not take Arcana's "one last thing". No man could stand against the force of this *slave*. No man should be required to.

"One more thing. Please," Arcana replied.

He could not resist such a pleasing voice. It frustrated him. It enticed him.

"What?" The fevered pressure behind his eyes increased. He heard a shuffle of a blanket falling away, a bare step on spongy white carpet, a whisper of still air, motes set whirling at Arcana's approach.

He sat very still. Throat tight. Heart stopped.

He saw the outline of the man standing before his bunk. He sensed it first. Then felt it. A hand, palm flat, pressed against his brow.

"Your skin is burning. And here I actually thought it would be cold," Arcana said.

He did not move. Blink. Or breathe.

Arcana said, "I just wanted to know that. Cold or hot. That is all."

The hand started to move away. Without conscious thought, Mordecai felt his arm move up, catch the thin wrist, hold it in place. He felt no returning pull or push, but just the right amount of relaxation. Arcana's hand stayed like a caress against his forehead.

Slowly, as if time were moving at a new and different rate, he felt Arcana's knee rest against the side of his bunk. Eventually his whole weight came to rest there, the mattress slightly dipping.

Mordecai swallowed once, and whispered, "I read your reports, especially the last ones, more than a dozen times."

"Good. Because they were my gifts to you. I don't know how to give in any other way." Arcana's voice was close. Mordecai could feel the light breath of it on his face.

"I don't know how to want without failing." The confession burst from his mouth without warning.

"Of course that is not true. You succeed at everything you do," came the man's reply.

"No. Not with lovers."

"Perhaps you haven't had the right one."

His back went stiff. He was not sure he would ever breathe right again. This man was leaning over him. This man who glowed. This man who had been indescribably tortured, opened, made raw and new. This Arlai slave.

"I can't—" He began. "I can't—"

"But what if you did?"

Something pressed his lips, firm, yielding, lips of a long lost boy, now two boys, one who had been caught and one who had escaped. Which was which?

Arcana pressed only slightly, with a graceful, external promise of more, and Mordecai leaned in. The lovely mouth opened. Slowly, he probed it with his tongue. Taste of spring. Taste of stars. The hand fell away from his forehead. His own let go of the narrow wrist. Now he reached out, encountering bare waist, hips, chest, all beauty amidst brief, still shocking glimpses of terror in his mind from this man's story—all of it surging toward him.

This was an Arlai slave.

This was a man.

But his mind still rushed. Was it right? Was it safe? Too much to contain.

They had not discussed anything. Preferences. Expectations. Wrongness. Rightness.

Mordecai liked plans. With impulsiveness, he was lost. He spoke suddenly, resolutely against the other man's lips. "I don't know what—"

Quickly, Arcana pressed words into his mouth. "You don't need to know. Feel."

But it was obvious Arcana wanted him to lead. To take charge. To top. His mind wanted to panic. His body pulled Arcana closer.

He ran fingers, barely touching, down the curve of his backside, finding the man already nude, and just like that Mordecai was fully hard.

He wrapped one arm about Arcana's waist, pressing in slightly to the soft skin, the bunched muscle. His other hand reached for his face.

When he caressed the jaw, Arcana pulled back a little. Mordecai froze.

"Don't think," Arcana whispered. "Keep going."

He caressed the side of Arcana's face, recalling he never had seen stubble on him, relishing the soft line, pushing his fingers through the usually errant, shining bangs. They were like liquid running over his hand.

Arcana sighed into his mouth. "Yes."

They were so close now, he could feel the man's eyelashes brushing his cheek, the hard cock pressing the sheet at his thighs.

Scent of flame on a cool night. Taste of earthen wind.

While Arcana was naked, he himself still wore shorts, and his own erection pressed against them, wanting free. It was sort of nice. One last confinement. Something he could still control. He made no effort to discard them.

When Arcana made a move to push them down with one hand, Mordecai's hand trailed through his cool hair and over his chest and belly, pushing Arcana's hand away.

"I see," Arcana said.

One step away, he was. Still tethered to a last proper vestment, as if his shorts symbolized the ship, the bunk, his body.

The hooded man came after him, then mysteriously turned away. The snow cave enfolded him.

I can't be caught. I can't be lost.

The strong hands of Arcana circled about his shoulders, his chest. He bucked up.

Arcana met him with equal force.

Nims on the deck. "We only got nine, sir."

Lost men. Lost boys. Broken from the stars.

Arcana whispered into his ear. "Let me. Let me."

It was confusing and wonderful. Nothing made sense. Yet everything had meaning.

Arcana's hand moved down again. Cupped him through the cloth.

He let him.

He closed his eyes tight. Saw green.

Come ahead.

Whiteness flashed behind his eyelids.

Purity expressed.

This had to be so new for Arcana in a way. Mordecai was no Arlai.

With hands they explored. Contours of tendon, rib, spine, buttock. The softness of fingertips, eyelids kissed, earlobes suckled. The dusting of hair on thighs tickled them.

Arcana was between his legs now, hand pulling the seam of his shorts at his thigh, stretching the elastic material back, letting Mordecai escape without letting go completely, allowing the shorts to remain. Arcana said, "I will not remove them. Just reveal."

He felt his cock become exposed to the air along the cushioning seam of cotton. Arcana pressed the edge of it up and over Mordecai's genitals, leaned down and began to lick.

Mordecai's whole body jerked, then settled to a slow tremble. He did not realize that for some time now he had been again clinging to the sheet's edge. It was off him now, pushed aside, but his left hand twisted within it. He bent his left knee. Pulled it up. Arcana's mouth, smooth, wet, teased with luscious fervor. He was already overcome, the white euphoria pouring through him like he'd never known before. Lips closed over him. He cried out when they moved down his shaft. The suction sweeter than the rush of all his successes, all control. More pure than any experience he'd ever had with another lover.

He cried out a second time, and his other hand found Arcana's velvet-soft hair. He thought he would come right then, but a moment later Arcana lifted off him and crawled naked into his arms, rubbing against him, nipping his throat, jaw, cheeks. Owning his lips again.

He wanted to float in that space with Arcana in his arms. Forever. Just like that. This precious man. His arms around him.

What was happening?

But he knew. He whispered. "I have wanted you so badly."

"I thought so. And then I wasn't sure. You are unflappable in your denial."

The end of that reply was muffled in another kiss. To drown in touch and taste. To be blinded by this high. Arcana was so beautiful Mordecai wished he could have a light to see the coppery, slippery skin, the power behind the gentle amber eyes. And yet he liked the blind explorations. The newness of it. The way the darkness made this like an illicit fantasy, a secret encounter.

For a long time, the kissing was a huge distraction. But urgencies climbed. Blood burned. Mordecai wanted to touch

Arcana and reached between them, no longer needing the grounding force of the sheet. Arcana moved to accommodate him, and Mordecai's first caress of the man's stiff flesh drawn tight up against his abdomen was hot, slightly slick, impressive. The energy of it went straight into him. His own cock throbbed, still caught between his thigh and the seam of his shorts.

He did not ask for more.

Arcana seemed to have lost his voice. Again.

Slowly, he urged the man forward and over him until Arcana's cock bobbed against Mordecai's face. He took it into his mouth, tasting salt, and a hint of tangy soap. More than anything, he wanted to give this man pleasure. He wanted to drink him up, have him, own him. For the moment, yes. Own him.

He used his hands to stroke. Arcana helplessly thrust, and Mordecai felt him twist back as he groaned aloud and came. It was everything he could want. Liquid. Quenching. Rich. A more tangible report this time.

He could feel the cock spasm again and again. He heard Arcana moan.

He wanted more. He suckled the stiff cock until he drank every drop. He loved all the textures, the ease of the foreskin moving up and down, the shudder of Arcana in afterglow sensitivity.

Amazingly, Arcana's cock did not go completely soft.

Finally, Arcana moved back, settling his bottom against Mordecai's still straining shaft, and began to move back and forth. He felt his cock caught up in the crease, probing.

Voice in a rush, "I did not prepare for this. I don't have—"

"Shh!" Arcana put his palm down on Mordecai's mouth. Almost a slap. His other hand reached between them and took Mordecai's cock in slick wetness.

"What?"

"Saliva works."

Arcana must have been wetting his hand all this time. And himself. It wasn't long before Arcana steered Mordecai's now slick cock to the entrance to his body and pushed down. The entry happened with slickness and ease. Saliva might evaporate quickly, but that wasn't an issue. Mordecai was not gong to last long.

Arcana rode him. It felt like the grandest dance. As if their bodies had known each other before. Had been waiting. It wasn't true, of course, but Mordecai wanted the illusion.

Warmth. Firmness. The clasp. The grasp. Arcana moved up and down, taking him, twisting a little, driving him to the brink until he could not breathe. He came hard. It lasted and lasted.

Arcana fell onto him, and wetness splashed between them as the young man came a second time. Mordecai grasped him in a strong embrace.

When he slipped out of Arcana's body he was still half-hard. This wasn't over. For the first time in his life with any lover, Mordecai forgot to wonder who was in control.

When he caught his breath, he nuzzled Arcana's head, kissing his glossy hair. Arcana folded into his arms, almost curling.

Arcana whispered, "I thought I knew."

That statement could have so many meanings. "Knew what?"

"That you could—" He stopped.

"Want you?" Mordecai finished the thought.

The silken head nodded against his chest.

"Give you back your purity?" Mordecai asked.

Another nod.

"Love you?"

"I would not dare to presume."

Mordecai turned in the bed, pushing Arcana onto his back, putting his face so close to his he could feel their breaths mingle. "Ah," he said. "But I very well could."

"Come ahead, then, Captain," said Arcana in his golden voice.

Epilogue

Arcana's brown hair flashed in the brilliant sunlight of the summer resort. The ocean glowed emerald green, the ebony beach sand soft as the powder of stardust.

Mordecai watched him come dripping from the waves like a god newly transformed to human. Arcana wore only pale blue trunks that left little to the imaginations. He plopped on the towel before Mordecai's chair, and stretched out his tanned body in a pose of utter contentment.

They had decided to honeymoon on Alioth 2. Six weeks of pleasure and bliss. Six weeks alone to learn more of each other's habits and cravings and hearts.

Arcana turned onto his side, facing the water. The scars on his back still concerned Mordecai, and sometimes he felt a pinch inside to see them, though they were quite faded and did not pain Arcana at all. The nightmares were gone, at least, and Arcana had eyes only for Mordecai.

"Cai," Arcana said. "I'm hungry."

"We have reservations at 7 for the steak house."

Arcana turned his head, and his damp hair curved across one eye, endearing. "Not that kind of hunger."

Mordecai's body heated from the inside, more powerful than the alien sun overhead. After months of courtship and living together, and then finally making their commitment, he'd learned that while he appeared to be the dominant one in their relationship, always on top so to speak, he was never really the one in charge.

Now, as he stood and held out his hand, he met Arcana's sweet eyes. Arcana reached up until their palms met, and Mordecai lifted him to his feet.

Hand in hand, bare feet sinking in the dark sand as they walked, they headed back to the cooler shadows of their suite where blue crystal decanters of the finest wine awaited them, where low green light emanated from the walls, and where their bed, soft and white as the purity of love welcomed them into its embrace.

(end)

Dear Reader:

Thank you for reading this darker sci fi/fantasy erotic romance.

I worked hard on putting honest emotions into this book. I put myself in the place of someone who might want what I can't imagine wanting, and then the writing was almost like channeling. The characters told me what they feared, and what they desired.

The subjects of abduction, non-con, and Stockholm Syndrome were very hard subjects to tackle. I read autobiographical books by real people who went through real ordeals of abduction, rape and captivity. These books gave me varying ideas of how people might handle such trauma, and no two people handled their ordeals the same. Learning this gave me the freedom to explore my characters as they demanded their story be told.

Also, with me, you're never going to get pat labels or definitions of roles. First and foremost, I am always true to my characters.

I really meditated hard on Mordecai and Arcana, and listened to them in my mind. I focused in on my daydreaming of this dark tale, and let it play, and tweaked it as it needed it.

For me, the result exceeded my expectations.

If you enjoyed this, you might also enjoy subscribing to my newsletter to receive news about new projects and sales. I put it out about six to eight times a year. I always have sales and freebies to offer readers both from myself and other authors I enjoy reading. If you subscribe at the link below, you can get a free copy of my book "Letters to an Android".

Happy Reading!
Wendy Rathbone

Contact links for Wendy:

Amazon author page: https://www.amazon.com/Wendy-Rathbone/e/B00B0O9BMS/ref=dp_byline_cont_ebooks_1

Facebook: https://www.facebook.com/wendy.rathbone.3

Blog: http://wendyrathbone.blogspot.com/

Newsletter sign up (you get a free copy of the critically acclaimed "Letters to an Android"): https://www.instafreebie.com/free/3ErH0

About Wendy Rathbone

I love to write. I have this thing about words and how they are used to describe beauty, love, and all the things that open us up inside to our true self, our power. Words do that for me. They make me happy. The new moon smiling, the sadness of a fallen feather at dusk, predatory eyes gazing through smoke.

The reason I write romance these days is because the overwhelming power of falling in love (which has been proven to heal even cancer) is a game-changer. It makes sad people instantly happy. It makes bleak reality look sun-warmed and friendly again.

I have written in all genres: scifi, fantasy, horror, paranormal, contemporary, erotica, romance. My poetry has won awards, publishing contracts, and was recently nominated for a Pushcart. A fiction story of mine won Writers of the Future. My fantasy/horror fiction and poetry has received honorable mentions from esteemed editor Ellen Datlow in "Years Best Fantasy and Horror". I am a hybrid writer, publishing both indie (under my press name Eye Scry Designs) and with publishers, most recently with Dreamspinner Press.

I keep coming back to romance. Gay romance. Male/male romance. Maybe it was the wonderful start I got when I was very young in Star Trek slash fanfiction. Something about that stuck. The idea of two men falling in love in a society that has winced at that sort of thing for far too long (when in ancient times and other cultures it is considered normal) is alluring. The forbidden is imminently appealing and erotic to me. Many of my themes involve abduction, pleasure slavery, indentured servitude, imprisonment. It's like, with my writing, I'm constantly breaking out of some self-imposed cage and letting my wings unfurl until I can finally fly.

This is why I write. This is what makes me burn.

All my books are available on Kindle and Create Space. So if you have the urge, go take a look. See what's on the shelf.

Love to you all!
Wendy Rathbone

Ganymede: Abducted by the Gods
Wendy Rathbone

Sold by his father
Abducted against his will.

My name is Ganymede, and I have been betrayed.

Every boy my age dreams of leaving home to embark on a noble adventure, but never does any boy imagine it happening as it did to me. On the evening of my 18th naming day, when I expected no more than a chalice of wine and a few drunken flirtations to tempt my innocence, I was instead sold by my father to the god, Zeus - not because of anything particular I had ever done or said, but solely because I am considered beautiful among mortals, and my father found more value in a few gold coins than in the well-being of his youngest son.

To be honest, I never believed in the gods, but my lack of belief held no power in Olympus or on Earth. Now under Zeus's influence, I am kept drunk on ambrosia in the sun-lit halls of the immortals, alternately amazed and horrified at the power these beings hold over others, and how darkly they influence the progress of humanity itself. How very much I want to hate Zeus for kidnapping me, and yet he shows me mostly kindness, even on that fateful night when we shared a bed for the first time. Kindness, yes, but also a godly and unyielding refusal to take no for an answer... probably because he could read my ambrosia-fevered curiosity as much as my naive, inexperienced terror. He owns me, after all, just as he owns everything else, so perhaps it never occurred to him that a captive and a slave might not make the best of lovers.

Throughout my time at Olympus - who's to say how long I've been here, for time on Olympus is not the same as that on Earth - the only thing that gives me hope comes to me in dreams and visions. His name is Sable and he is a magnificent shape-shifter in the form of a giant raven. When he first spoke to me in my mind it was with a resonance unlike any I had ever known - his mind and mine sounding a single note together, a song without words, a promise of freedom, a glimpse of some distant but very real possibility of this thing we humans call Love. But now he is silent. Perhaps I dreamed his voice. Perhaps I have finally lost my mind...

———

This male/male romance is a sensual, fantastic and alternate myth, where captivity leads to transformation, immortality and finally love.

"Fans of "*The Song of Achilles*" by Madeline Miller, and "*Captive Prince*" by C.S. Pacat will especially enjoy Rathbone's version of the Ganymede's myth." – A.J., blog reviewer

www.eyescrypublications.com
**Also on Amazon or
order from your favorite bookseller.**

Turn Left at November

**Poems by
Wendy Rathbone**

Visit realms of diamond rain, dust-folk lands and valleys of curses and shame. Reside in the burning moonships of dream, the silt of stars, the asphyxiation of the waking day. Meet the golden android who houses your soul. Journey through tatters of stardust down roads of sorrow. Find hope in planets of candles and crazy-eyed mermen. There you will meet November in these rich and evocative poems by Wendy Rathbone.

Unmaking Autumn

*Out at the excavation site
where they are taking apart autumn
leaf by fabled leaf
the searchlights try to catch us
putting the eyes back into the pumpkins
the moon back in the witch-shaped sky
We steal blood kisses*
behind the naked apple orchards.

www.eyescrypublications.com
Also on Amazon or
order from your favorite bookseller

LETTERS TO AN ANDROID

Wendy Rathbone

Cobalt is a created human, vat grown and born adult, with no human rights and indentured to serve others for the duration of his life. Liyan is a young man with wanderlust in his eyes, embarking on a career that takes him to the furthest regions of space. The two become unlikely friends and create a memorable long-distance correspondence. Through Liyan, Cobalt gets to explore the universe, living vicariously through his friend's wave transmissions. A strong bond develops between them that not even the stars can put asunder.

Now you know an android who writes poetry.

This is all your fault. Did you not read my last wave telling you extracurricular activities for my kind are discouraged? Of course this is harmless and strangely enjoyable and does not necessarily require me to leave the hotel. Pel would not care if I wrote lines of equations or nonsensical juxtaposed words. As long as the act does not bring my mental state into question.

However, in history, poetry is often written by the rebels.

So we can keep this to ourselves.

Let me know about your lieutenant's test.

And to give you peace of mind, I never believed you observed me as anything other than human.

Some people are and always will be hateful bigots. Most people are simply uncomfortable in speaking to "property." And anyway, friendship, like poetry, is also discouraged.

Your friend,
Cobalt

SCOUNDREL
Wendy Rathbone
A male/male romance

Antares is a willing sex slave, trained in the harems of Anada since the age of 18, and owned by a wealthy master who spoils his slaves. But all that changes when Empire soldiers invade Antares' world and he is taken away from the only life he's ever known.

In a colonized galaxy where starships are as common as houseflies, and a dark Empire seeks to control thousands of civilized worlds, there are those who fall through the cracks and refuse to be conquered, including the pirate, Slate, and his crew.

Out in the darkness of the unknown, among Empire soldiers and scoundrels, will bad fates befall Antares and his fellow captive companions?

Will Slate finally find the love he's been looking for his whole life?

Can Slate and Antares ever see eye to eye?

A male/male romance to end all male/male romances!

www.eyescrypublications.com
Also on Amazon or
order from your favorite bookseller.

LACE
Wendy Rathbone

Lace is a being from another dimension on Earth. He cannot die and humans call his kind "vampire" and declare war on them.

Firi is a human military soldier, a trained guard, who has met Lace twice in his young life and formed a bond with him.

In a world where humans and vampires are arch enemies, where vampires are eradicated in horrible ways, where being a vampire-lover means a death sentence, can Firi and Lace ever find each other again and explore the feelings they have for each other?

Will Lace be able escape his government prison, and the amnesia that keeps him from accessing his true powers?

Can Firi, the boy he met in the woods ten years ago, ever hope to help him?

A male/male romance about secrets that can get you killed, impossible rescues, and old lovers who cannot be trusted.

The Foundling
by Wendy Rathbone

Diego is a powerful man with a tragic past. Out on the expansive ocean in his private yacht, he discovers a beautiful and mysterious man adrift on a raft, near death. The bond that forms between them in the aftermath of Alec's rescue is one of fierce passion, though lacking in trust. Can they make it work, or will Alec's amnesia bring forth secrets so disturbing as to tear them apart? A passionately erotic love story of desire and darkness, exquisite and explicit.

I can see his struggle between gratitude and uneasiness. He is buffeted by all things new and strange. He does not know where he is from, who he is or what happened to him. He does not know me. There has not been enough time to transition between strangers and friendship.

This isolation of his is something I can identify with, but it is also a feeling no one can help him with until or unless he gets his own life back. And his memory.

If that doesn't happen, then it will take time for him to build a new life. He is polite to me, even friendly, but even a night together during a storm with his arms wrapped tight around my waist doesn't calm the surge I see inside him, the emptiness, the loss, possibly even panic. That night may have reinforced some trust in me, but so far not enough for him to completely relax.

He seeks me out, though. That's something. He sits by me at dinner when he can have any seat of his choosing. I watch him closely when he does not realize it. At dinner the following night after we had only 'slept' together, and before we go to bed again in separate rooms, I notice everything about him, how he moves, the way the air warms when he is closer to me, the dry sheen of his lips as they part for more air when he is reacting to something, or speaking, or eating.

His hands still shake. Anyone else might not notice because he keeps them clasped into fists at his sides or, while sitting, pressed tight to his lap.

I spend another fretful night alone. I dream restlessly, wild, loud and colorful visions I cannot recall at all as soon as my eyes open. All I know is the dreams leave me unfulfilled, impatient.

www.eyescrypublications.com
Also on Amazon or from your favorite bookseller.

SONS OF NEVERLAND
an erotic vampire novel
by Della Van Hise

"The virtuosity shown here is only the beginning of a pyrotechnic talent unfolding into the hidden dimensions of the human and nonhuman spirit."
                    -Jacqueline Lichtenberg

Set against a backdrop of contemporary culture, *Sons of Neverland* explores the universal questions of love, sex and death - the three most crucial challenges every human being must face. Stefan London is a grieving man, suffering through the loss of his young daughter. When he goes to a science fiction convention in the hopes of meeting her friends, he encounters instead a young man who is dangerously seductive and undeniably magical. Lured into the night by Dimitri, Stefan soon discovers himself in a world where vampires are real, and the world is not at all what he has always believed, and immortality is only a deep red kiss away.

But the price of eternal life is high, and as his handsome maker warns, "Through my blood you will learn a secret which will compel you to live forever, yet a secret so sinister it will haunt you for that same eternity."

The secret will haunt you, too.

———

"This book zones on the question of immortality. However, this is not just the decadent historical immortality of the long-lived vampire, it is immortality as a change in one's perception. This is the story behind the story, delivered by characters that are hyper-real - each one loaded with symbolism. *Sons of Neverland* will have you filled, even brimming over with the sense of Mysterium Tremendum et Fascinans. Go there for a full helping of the numinous." (A Reviewer on Amazon)

Prince of Umberlight
Alexis Fegan Black

"If Prince of Umberlight doesn't rattle your cage, you're more dead than the undead!" **-Night Readers**

Thorn may be an 800 year old vampire, but he does not possess the ability to create others of his kind, and so he is cursed to fall in love with mortals, only to watch them grow old and die. Torn by grief, Thorn denounces his immortality and enters into a comatose oblivion for decades. When he awakens, he is no longer in London, but finds himself in a world spun into being by his own desires - a world where Time and Death do not exist, a world where it is forever autumn, where the Parish of Shadows and the River of Stars become his home. It is in this world of Umberlight that he meets Atom - an interloper into his private sanctuary, but also an impudent imp who is destined to reveal to Thorn the three dangerous elements a vampire must possess in order to become a Creator.

The Art of Brutality.
Submission to Dark Desire.
Love.

YEAR OF THE RAM
Della Van Hise

Year of the Ram was described by one reviewer as... "A spacefaring gay romance full of love, angst, and longing."

Only after Star Commander Morgan Diego becomes an exile as a result of a Galaxy Corps political blunder does he begin to realize how much he valued the companionship of his second in command - the mysterious Lucien, an Alfarian who is more elven than human, with peculiar powers & abilities which begin to unfold as he, too, realizes what he has lost.

Separated by circumstance from his former life, Morgan is thrust into a world where he must survive by his wits. When he meets a peculiar little old man calling himself Kim Le, Morgan finds himself in a situation where he is required to master The Art - not only a form of human & extraterrestrial martial arts, but a way of living and being that will alter his life forever.

At the temple, he is introduced to his new teacher, another Alfarian who begins to steal his heart - a heart which is already promised to Lucien. Torn and conflicted, Morgan struggles with the world he left behind and the world he now inhabits.

Beginning to believe he may never again return to his ship and to the friends and loved ones he left behind, he is all the more frustrated and heartbroken when a new Master arrives at the temple: a man to whom Morgan is immediately drawn both mentally and physically, a man who is strikingly familiar... yet utterly alien.

Year of the Ram is a fully-fleshed novel, approximately 97000 words, with a focus on the love story and romance angle. Set against a science fiction milieu, it explores the infinite possibilities of the human and alien heart. Sexual content is explicit, though is not the primary focus of the novel.

For those who like a romance that forces its characters to contemplate the ecstasies AND the agonies of love... you will enjoy *Year of the Ram* immensely.

www.eyescrypublications.com
Also on Amazon or
order from your favorite bookseller.

All of our titles are available directly from our website, on Amazon, or may be ordered from most booksellers. Thanks for reading us!

Eye Scry Publications
A Visionary Publishing Company
www.eyescrypublications.com